CRIME & CO.

Borgo Press Books by S. Fowler Wright

Arresting Delia: An Inspector Cleveland Classic Crime Novel
The Attic Murder: An Inspector Combridge & Mr. Jellipot Classic Crime Novel
The Bell Street Murders: An Inspector Combridge & Mr. Jellipot Classic Crime Novel
Beyond the Rim: A Lost Race Fantasy
Black Widow: A Classic Crime Novel
The Capone Caper: Mr. Jellipot vs. the King of Crime: A Classic Crime Novel
Crime & Co.: An Inspector Cleveland Classic Crime Novel
Dawn: A Novel of Global Warming
Dead by Saturday: An Inspector Cleveland Classic Crime Novel
Dream; or, The Simian Maid: A Fantasy of Prehistory (Marguerite Cranleigh #1)
Elfwin: An Historical Novel of Anglo-Saxon Times
The End of the Mildew Gang: An Inspector Cauldron Classic Crime Novel (Mildew Gang #3)
Four Callers in Razor Street: An Inspector Combridge & Mr. Jellipot Classic Crime Novel
The Hanging of Constance Hillier: An Inspector Cleveland Classic Crime Novel
The Hidden Tribe: A Lost Race Fantasy
The Jordans Murder: An Inspector Combridge & Mr. Jellipot Classic Crime Novel
The King Against Anne Bickerton: A Classic Crime Novel
The Mildew Gang: An Inspector Cauldron Classic Crime Novel (Mildew Gang #1)
Murder in Bethnal Square: An Inspector Combridge & Mr. Jellipot Classic Crime Novel
The Police and the Public: Some Thoughts on the British System of Justice
Post-Mortem Evidence: An Inspector Combridge & Mr. Jellipot Classic Crime Novel
The Return of the Mildew Gang: An Inspector Cauldron Classic Crime Novel (Mildew Gang #2)
The Rissole Mystery: An Inspector Combridge & Mr. Jellipot Classic Crime Novel
The Screaming Lake: A Lost Race Fantasy
The Secret of the Screen: An Inspector Combridge & Mr. Jellipot Classic Crime Novel
Spiders' War: A Novel of the Far Future (Marguerite Cranleigh #3)
Three Witnesses: A Classic Crime Novel
Too Much for Mr. Jellipot: An Inspector Combridge & Mr. Jellipot Classic Crime Novel
The Vengeance of Gwa: A Fantasy of Prehistory (Marguerite Cranleigh #2)
Was Murder Done? A Classic Crime Novel
Who Murdered Reynard? A Classic Crime Novel
The Wills of Jane Kanwhistle: An Inspector Combridge & Mr. Jellipot Classic Crime Novel
With Cause Enough?: An Inspector Combridge & Mr. Jellipot Classic Crime Novel

CRIME & CO.

AN INSPECTOR CLEVELAND CLASSIC CRIME NOVEL

by

S. FOWLER WRIGHT

WRITING AS "SYDNEY FOWLER"

THE BORGO PRESS

An Imprint of Wildside Press LLC

MMIX

CONTENTS

CHAPTER I.

THE caretaker at Bodmin House was also the lift-attendant. He received Major Cattell-Pratt with affability, for it was to his financial advantage that all the offices should be let, the cleaning of them, which was under his wife's charge, being their principal source of income. He had a keen eye for a good tenant, and he was prompt to call his daughter from the basement to take his place, when they had ascended to the third floor, and he led the way along the corridor to the vacant room.

This room was on the left, at the far end, and two doors before reaching it they must pass the one in which the Major was the more actively interested.

He noticed, as he loitered a few paces behind, while the caretaker paused to select the right key from his bunch, that the sign writers had done their work on door:

BULFWIN'S SYNDICATE, LTD. Registered Office

He was somewhat puzzled on reading this, and turned it over in a slow mind, while he absently surveyed the interior of the vacant office which the caretaker had now opened to his inspection.

He saw that, if a company were already registered, the business which Mr. Trentham had in hand must have been maturing for some time, but he was more puzzled by the name, which did not give the impression of solid respectability and deep-rooted opulence which was usual to that gentleman's selected titles.

Well, if it were registered, there would still be time to visit Somerset House and gain some interesting information before he went home to tea.

"I don't think I like this back view. The other wall comes too close," he said, as he gazed out of an unwashed window to a restricted view of white washed bricks. "Can't you find me a front one of about the same size?"

"Not just now, sir. Most gentlemen prefer the back rooms. They say they're so much quieter."

That was what he always said when he offered a back room. It is less certain that any gentleman had said it before him. When he let a front one, he dwelt on the advertising value of the windows, which could be clearly seen by those who rode Fenchurch Street on the bus-tops, for this side of the building overlooked that thoroughfare.

The Major was unimpressed.

"I should much prefer a front room, if you have one to offer. It ought to be more cheerful than this. Have you one you could show me?"

The man did not rise to the bait. "No, sir, I'm afraid they're all let. There's Mr. Crockford's as may come vacant at March. But he's a rather particular gentleman. I shouldn't like to be showing it you, if he came in."

"Haven't you got one I could see? I might take this for the time, if I liked the front ones, and move across at the first vacancy."

"There's one here, sir, that's just let, but they haven't moved in. There's no harm in you seeing it."

Neither, thought the Major, was there much good, if it were as empty as the words implied, but he had to keep smelling round at this game, never knowing when he might discover something that would be useful at last.

He was not keenly alert to so unpromising an opportunity, and his glance wandered along the corridor to where a man was just emerging from the lift at the farther end, so that he did not look into the room as the key turned, and the caretaker pushed open the door.

"*Oh, my God.*" It was a cry of utter horror, as the man drew back, pulling the door shut again as he did. The Major's glance came sharply upon him. He was visibly trembling. He spoke with a shaking jaw.

"Oh, sir, there's a man—it's all blood…."

Major Cattell-Pratt pushed him aside. He opened the door and looked in. He gazed for a moment in I silence, and then closed it again.

"You'd better leave it as it is and telephone for the once at once."

He turned to find that Mr. Mortimer Trentham was at elbow.

Mr. Trentham was a tall man, rather heavily-built, but not flabby. He had an air of commanding geniality.

He had evidently come to enter that office, and he stood as though expecting the Major to give way before him.

But Cattell-Pratt stood his ground.

8

"If you please," said Mr. Trentham, somewhat imperiously, "I have an appointment with Mr. Bulfwin."

"I don't think I would go in there. There is a man dead."

Mr. Trentham looked surprised and startled, but he did not withdraw from his purpose. He said:

"Are you from the police?"

"Oh, no," the Major answered innocently. "But I think the caretaker's gone to call them." For that individual had made a hurried dash into an adjoining office, and his quavering voice was already audible at the telephone.

"Then perhaps you'll stand aside." The Major hesitated. Having met Mr. Trentham thus, it was not his policy to quarrel, but he knew the importance of such an investigation being commenced in a systematic way.

"I don't think we ought to interfere," he said, "till they come. But, of course, you can look in if you like. You may know who it is. It's a beastly sight, anyhow."

He stepped aside, and Mr. Trentham opened the door.

The floor of the room, which was otherwise spread from wall to wall with pools and splashes of blood, and in the midst a man lay as he had fallen forward, his face turned sideways from the floor, and distorted as by agony or rage. His hands were closed convulsively. On either side, from the lower part of his body, spread a wide pool of curdled blood. There could be no doubt of his death.

Mr. Trentham did not enter, nor draw back.

The Major, watching closely, thought that he was paler than before, but he did not lose his composure.

"That's Bulfwin," he said. "It's a case for the police, right enough. Poor fellow. It's a bad day for me. I had my secretary drowned at Brighton this morning, or I should have been here hours ago...and now this."

He fell silent, perhaps regretting that he had said so much to a stranger.

The Major uttered a conventional expression of sympathy, and became aware that he was being scrutinized closely.

"Did you know him?" Mr. Trentham asked, with an abruptness which may have been intentional.

"No. I happened to be here when the caretaker made the discovery, so I suppose I ought to wait, and tell the police how it occurred. Did you?"

"Yes," Trentham answered shortly. Conversation ceased.

CHAPTER II.

IT seemed a surprisingly short time, even to those who waited in the passage, before the caretaker appeared again, leading a police sergeant, with two attendant constables, to the scene of the murder.

The sergeant opened the door, and took a step or two within the room, giving it a swiftly comprehensive professional glance, and then drew back, closing it again.

He spoke to the constables. "Inspector Cleveland will be here in a few minutes. You must let no one enter in the meantime."

He turned his attention to the two men who waited in the passage.

"I don't know how much you know about this, gentlemen; but I must ask you kindly to wait here till the Inspector arrives."

The Major was quite content to remain, but he was sufficiently aware of the limitations of a police-sergeant's powers to know that he was asking more than he could demand. He was willing that Trentham should see him in conflict with the police, rather than suspect him of complicity with them.

He had the wit to say brusquely,

"I'm not going to wait here, Sergeant; I've got something better to do."

The man looked at him doubtfully. Probably, he might have no information to give which would be of value. He did not suspect him of any responsibility for the crime. But he thought that the Inspector would expect him to detain these men, if possible, till his own arrival.

Trentham interposed "I don't think this gentleman knows anything about the matter, Sergeant. He just happened to be in the passage when the caretaker looked in. But I know the dead man, and may be able to give you some information. I will wait, if it isn't too long."

"Thank you, sir," said the Sergeant; and then to the Major, "I'm sure it would be, better to wait; but if you can't, I must have your name and address."

The Major pulled out his card-case, beginning to move along the passage as he did so.

Mr. Trentham, watching, saw a card pass, but could not hear what was said. He saw the two men stand talking for a moment at the lift-head, and then the Major returned.

"He says I shall get him into trouble if I go, and fit won't be more than ten minutes, so I've promised to stay that long."

What he had said to the Sergeant had ended with the words, "Tell him particularly not to know me and not to be too polite."

The man went down, and waited to intercept Inspector Cleveland as he entered the building.

Having sufficiently explained his return, the Major relapsed into a silence about which his sister would have said that there was nothing unusual.

The two constables stood stolidly by the door. They would probably report any conversation which they might overhear, but there would be no opening gambit from them.

Mr. Trentham did not speak. Whether or not he had had reason to expect the tragedy which lay behind the guarded door, he may have had sufficient to occupy his mind in the interval before he must give the information which he had offered.

As to the Major, his mental-processes were naturally slow, and he was glad of the quiet interval to speculate upon the possibilities of this unexpected development.

It will be seen that it was not a chatty group which was joined, after about five minutes, by another would-be caller at Mr. Bulfwin's office.

This was a small, slim, active man, with a quick, light walk, who appeared from the stair-head, having ignored the lift, and stopped with an expression of surprise at the silent group before the door.

"Gee! What's up?" he inquired, with a very slight American accent.

The voice was soft, almost girlish in quality. The face was youthful, and brought the same word to the Major's mind. Boyish. No, girlish. Not effeminate, certainly. Girlish was the word.

And yet—there was at that moment a hardness of alert grey eyes, and of a rather close-lipped mouth, which challenged the first impression with more formidable, if not more sinister possibilities.

"All struck dumb?" he went on. "What's the game? I want to see Mr. Bulfwin."

The quick eyes moved from one to another in impatient query, and Mr. Trentham answered:

"I'm sorry to say, Mr. Kingsley, that Bulfwin has been murdered, or committed suicide. We are waiting for a police officer who will take charge of the case."

Mr. Kingsley looked more surprised at the use of his own name than at the news of Mr. Bulfwin's decease.

He said, "I don't reckon we've met before...I suppose you're Trentham?"

Mr. Trentham looked somewhat annoyed at this familiar designation.

He answered, with a more distant formality, "I don't think we have, but I recognized Mr. Kingsley from the description that I had received." His hand indicated the door which divided them from the dead man.

"Oh, he did, did he?" was Mr. Kingsley's response. "I wonder what's cracked him up. He was all head-in-air when I saw him yesterday. Didn't seem worried a bean.

Mr. Kingsley coming had certainly livened the conversational atmosphere, and Mr. Trentham appeared to be about to reply, when the lift-door was heard once more at the passage end, and Inspector Cleveland advanced briskly, with the caretaker, and a gentleman with a bag, whose profession was sufficiently indicated.

The Major was not unacquainted with Inspector Cleveland. He had, indeed, been thinking how fortunate it was that he had returned from Brighton that morning. A stroke of good fortune for both, as it would enable them to follow the case together without any gap, or the interference of other officers.

But the Inspector had received his message. He glanced over little group with an equal indifference.

"Now, gentlemen," he said, with a tone of official curtness which discounted the courtesy of the actual words, "if you've got any information to give me, I shall be pleased to have it as soon as I've made an inspection. But we mustn't ask you to stand like this. Caretaker, can't you find a room where you can give these gentlemen seats?"

The caretaker led the way at once to the office from which he had telephoned.

"This way, gentlemen, if you please. I don't suppose Mr. Crockford'll be coming in, and I'm sure he won't mind if he does."

The Major observed that his fear of that individual had been signally reduced by the stronger emotions excited by the catastrophe. They filed into the room, and took Mr. Crockford's chairs—Trentham, Kingsley, and himself.

Here they sat for about ten minutes, observing that one of the constables had been stationed at the door, and in some doubt as to the degree of the detention which they were experiencing.

The conversational impulse which Inspector Cleveland had interrupted appeared to have died. They sat in silence till he entered the room, and dismissed the constable, closing the door behind him.

Inspector Cleveland had his limitations. He would have been incapable of reconstructing a crime, and the life history of everyone connected with it, from the concentrated study of a half-burnt match. But he had been engaged in the investigation of crime for over twenty years without any serious error being recorded against him, unless it were in regard to the hanging of Constance Hillier,[1] and in that case the evidence had been of such a nature that his conduct had been approved by his superiors, and only criticized before the harder tribunal of his own thoughts. His detractors had been heard to say that he had been fortunate in being occupied upon cases which had not required any exceptional ability for their elucidation. His admirers (if any) might have retorted that his efficiency tended to make the difficult easy, and that many of his cases would have appeared more abstruse had they been handled by one of showier but more superficial attributes.

He was a man of a somewhat unobtrusive efficiency, which is a first requirement for success in his profession. He was of medium height, of medium build. His slightly grizzled hair was neither dark nor light; his eyes were neither brown nor blue. He could have written a moderately accurate description of most men that he met for the first time, after an interval of several days, had he been required to do so. A man might travel with him in the same railway compartment for a month, and find a difficulty in remembering any definite feature or characteristic which he could describe with certainty.

Even the somewhat brusque official tone which he very commonly used was less than an established mannerism, and would change with circumstance into a more courteous, deferential or even convivial mode of address. He had never been known to utter a rash forecast, or an extreme opinion. He had not received the great benefit (as the Major would have judged it) of a University education,

---

[1] See *The Hanging of Constance Hillier*.

but he fulfilled many of the requirements of that gentleman's social code. No one would ever call him a crank.

"I'm afraid," he said, with a manner which was faintly apologetic, but in a tone of official decision, "that I shall have to trouble you all for statements of what you know of this matter. I'm not suggesting that any of you has any responsibility for it, but there's been murder done here not many hours ago. I understand that two of you knew the man, and had come to see him. Mr...."—he glanced at the Major's card—"Mr. Cattle-Pratt does not appear to have more than a very casual connection with the case, but I should like his account of how the office came to be opened when it did. If you would all come back to the Yard with me now, I might not detain you very long this afternoon."

The Major answered with an annoyance which was not entirely simulated. If he had asked that he should not be recognized, it was no reason for Cleveland pretending that he couldn't pronounce his name properly. He said that he had something else to do.

But his protest was ignored. The Inspector was talking to Mr. Trentham, who was expressing his willingness to give the police the benefit of such knowledge as he possessed.

The Inspector said little to Mr. Kingsley, or he to him. Perhaps a larger acquaintance with American than English police methods led that gentleman to suppose that he had no option but to obey their requirements. He said nothing, but appeared quite at ease, as the Inspector led the way to the descent of the lift, and to pack them in his waiting car.

CHAPTER III.

MR. KINGSLEY, being politely invited into a separate room on his arrival at Scotland Yard, found that he had a considerable period of leisure, during which he might have prepared his mind for the examination that was before him, but he did not appear to be greatly concerned upon that or any other preoccupation, endeavouring rather to engage a plainclothes officer, who was writing at a desk at the farther side of the room, in a desultory conversation which received little encouragement.

The Inspector entered the room with the Major behind him.

He indicated a cane chair against the farther wall.

"You can sit there, Mr. Pratt; I'll attend to you later," he said shortly. "Now, Mr. Kingsley, pull your chair up here."

He seated himself at a central table, indicating a position for Mr. Kingsley on the opposite side, and the other occupant of the room came over and sat at his left hand. He brought foolscap paper, prepared to take down the answers to the examination.

"What is your full name, Mr. Kingsley?"

"I'm not Kingsley rightly. My name's Lytton Kingsley Starr. Bulfwin called me Kingsley, not mister, and Trentham thinks I'm Mr. Kingsley, and so you go on guessing, and you guess wrong. That's for a start. Now Officer, listen here."

Mr. Starr put his elbows on the table, and leant forward with bright alert eyes staring straightly into those of the Inspector. "I saw this man yesterday afternoon, and you tell me he's murdered now. There's no loss in that.

"Well, I could tell you a good bit about him, though I can't say whether you'll find it much help. That's for you.

"But when I've told you all *I* know, there's two things you'll know sure. He's no loss, as I've said, and it's good to me that he's cracked up.

"I'm not a Britisher, and I don't know much of your London ways, but if you're trying a frame-up on me, I won't give you a word more I wouldn't risk the chair for a man like that. Get me?"

"We don't try frame-ups here, Mr. Starr. You're in a civilized country. I'll be quite frank with you. You are under suspicion, to the extent that everyone must be who has been in recent contact with the dead man, until we can put our hands on the murderer. But we do not wish to suspect anyone unjustly, and we therefore ask you to give us a statement of your connection with him, and of your movements during the time at which the murder must have occurred. If you're guilty, some of the questions I shall ask may not be easy to answer. I can't make you speak, but if you're innocent, it can only help you for us to know the truth."

"That mayn't be quite as sure as it sounds," Mr. Starr replied, with some scepticism. "But I don't think you could fix it on me if you tried. I don't even carry a gun in this country." He lifted a jacket to display a hip-pocket which was certainly empty.

"I didn't say he was shot," the Inspector replied very quietly.

"No; and you didn't say he was drowned. But you said he was killed, and killing mostly means gunning in our parts," was the ready answer, unperturbed by the slip, if such it were.

"Well, I'll tell you this," he went on. "Bulfwin came East to float a mine that was half his and half mine, and to sell a process that wasn't his at all, but that he'd been promised a corner in, if he pulled it off—"

"Wait a moment," said the Inspector, "we'd better have this down properly."

His assistant, who had been entering busily in a shorthand notebook, laid it down, and took pen and foolscap in anticipation of the statement which he was to write out.

"Easy there," said Starr, "what's the game? Your man's a stenographer, isn't he? If he's going to longhand all I say, we shall be here for a week."

"You must leave me to decide the form in which your statement is to be taken," said the Inspector, in his official voice. "You couldn't be expected to read Sergeant Grover's shorthand, and we can't ask you to sign anything you haven't read over first."

"If you think I'm going to sign anything here, Officer, you can guess again. There's a bit I can tell, if you want to know, and you can check it up how you like, but there's no signing for me."

"I shall certainly ask you to sign your statement, Mr. Starr. If you are proposing to tell me the truth, about which I don't wish to suggest any doubt, it's difficult to see why you should object. An unsigned statement has no value at all."

"Value for what?"

"Value as evidence."

"I'm not giving evidence, and if I do, it'll be in my own words. I'm giving information, if you want that; and if you don't, I'll go."

"Very well," said the Inspector, conceding the point, without allowing his annoyance to appear, "you can have it your own way, but it's better for you to see what we've got, and to have an opportunity of correcting any mistake."

"Then we'll leave it there," Mr. Starr answered easily. "I guess he's a clever guy at the job, and he might put my words down, or he might put his, but anyway I don't want to sit here for a week. If you get it wrong, and it won't check up straight, you can ask again.

"Now listen here, Officer. I'm not going to tell you who shot Bulfwin—you can call it drowned, if you like—for that's more than I know; but he's been near it before this, and you'll find a mark behind his left ear where a bullet cracked his skull three years ago. That came from a sage bush, and no one ever knew who pulled the gun, but about two hundred people could have made a good guess, and they'd have all guessed the same. They've not stopped offering to teach Joe Prescott to shoot straight yet. But I don't know who."

"Where's Joe Prescott now?"

"Likely he's asleep in his own shack, it not being daylight yet in his parts. He's not in England, if you mean that. Not as far as I know. Leastways, he was on Chickadee main street when I entrained for the boat. He wouldn't be that soft that he'd come here to shoot him up, when it might have been done a lot safer there, and less questions asked."

"What boat did you come on?"

Mr. Starr paused for one almost imperceptible instant before he answered.

"*Baltic*, from N'York. I landed Liverpool, a fortnight back, come Monday."

"Where are you staying?"

"I'll tell you that when you tell me that you'll leave me alone. I don't mean to find all my things turned inside out when I get back, and a bullet maybe put through my gun."

The Inspector looked puzzled.

"Don't get me?" Mr. Starr inquired, with a smile that broke through the hard brightness of his eyes for the first time. "Well, it mightn't be your way. But if some of our guys wanted to make a frame-up on me, and they got their hands on my gun, they'd soon fire a bullet through it that'd be the one that was cut out of the dead man, and there'd be the barrel-marks to prove whose gun had been busy in that room. They did it once too much last year, when it came out that the gun hadn't been bought *or made* at the shooting-date, and that's where they came apart."

"You seem to know about these things," the Inspector remarked, dryly enough. "But the real point is that you won't give your address. That's bound to be a black mark against you, and you might be surprised to know how soon we shall find that out in our own way—and I'll tell you straight that I *should* like to see that pistol, and if you know nothing of this murder, you might be a wiser man if you met us in a different way."

"Maybe so, and maybe not," Mr. Starr answered, confidently. "But what you want to know is why I was calling at Bulfwin's office yesterday, and again today, and that's a plain tale, and soon told.

"Well, my dad ran the hotel at Chickadee, when the first gold rush was on. He died there, twenty-two years back, two months before I was born. My mother'd gone East; it doesn't matter why. Chickadee went down after that, but she sold out when Dad died, and it didn't matter to her. Now it's up again, and she'd have done better to hold on, but she needed the money then, and it's maybe best as it was."

"Do you mean that you are only twenty-two, Mr. Starr?"

"That's so. Do I look a bit worn at the seams? Well, I'm not feeling any decay yet. Maybe I'd look younger if I'd lived easy, and lain soft. But that's out of this tale. When my mother died last fall, I went over a lot of old papers of Dad's that she'd most like never read, or understood if she did, and I found that he'd owned a half-share in a mining claim with a man named Peters. My mother *had* read that, for there were letters after that date, showing that they'd stopped working the claim—it was platinum, not gold—because it never paid. Always just a bit on the wrong side, at the price platinum was then. And then came a notice that Peters had sold out for $300 to this Bulfwin, who said he'd just hold on in case prices went up, and the mine wouldn't cost anything to keep. That didn't sound much for our share—"

"Our?"

"Mother's and mine."

"But your mother was dead."

"Well, it's just a manner of speaking. But I thought I'd go and have a look for myself, and I found that Bulfwin had started working that claim about four years before, and it was a busy place when I called in to see.

"Well, he allowed who I was easy enough, and showed me what he'd spent, which was a bit more than he'd got back, but the prospect looked fairly good. It's not what you'd call a rich claim, but it's a big one. There's no end to the dirt, if you can make it pay to wash.

"But I'd got something else in mind, and it turned out that he'd got the same thing.

"We had a talk the next day, and he said, 'I've heard tell that Peters had found a way of washing this dirt that'd cut the cost to half what it takes to get the ore now. There's a letter somewhere that he sold it to your dad. If you could find that, it might turn this mine to a good thing.'

"I said, 'That's about true.' I found the papers, which I don't think my mother had ever read. But it's not for washing out the ore. It's a new method of separating the metals, and it's likely others have found it out since that day, if it's any good. But it means machines, and a lot of power, and other things. They reckoned then that it needed $50,000 to make a start, and that's why nothing was ever done."

"'Then,' he said, 'it's a bigger thing than I thought, or it's just nothing at all,' and I said 'Yep' to that.

"Well, to make it short, we got a man I know from a mining college, and he went into those papers, and he said there was a fortune if it all worked out, as he thought it would, and he could tell us sure that it was a new thing.

"Now up to then I'd found Bulfwin square enough, and when he said he could get ten times the money for the mine and those papers and a straighter deal in London than anywhere else, I let him come—that was about six months ago—and gave him power to sell the mine for a good price, of which half was to be paid direct to my name in a Denver bank—that was what he proposed—and he was to get ten percent on whatever the process fetched, and the rest come to me in the same way.

"Well, there were those who called me a fool, but he'd been straight with me up to then, and I couldn't see how he could go wrong if he tried. There could be no sale without that money being paid to my name. But about three months ago, someone came on what was left of a dead man, who'd been shot in the back, and there was enough lying around to tell that it had been my pal from the mining college, and I remembered something that Bulfwin had begun to say, and then shut up, and I knew as sure as I sit here that he'd done him in when he left us, because he knew the process, and he wouldn't trust his word that he wouldn't split.

"When I'd worked that out, I came sure by the next boat. I'd have no dealings through him, if I could get here in time.

"Well, I was about ten days too late. He'd sold the mine for a fair price enough, and it seems that my share of the money'll be waiting for me at Denver when I get back; but he'd sold the process, *if it proved a success*, for just $10,000, to be paid in a year's time, when it'll be worth more like five millions if anything."

The Inspector had listened so far with little interruption, while his assistant's pencil moved swiftly to transcribe the crisp rapidity of Mr. Starr's narrative. But he interposed now to ask:

"If he were to get ten percent, I don't see how he scored by a bad sale."

"Well, he did. He was to be manager of this syndicate that Trentham started, at £5,000 a year for life, and be insured for £50,000."

"Payable at his death?" The Inspector's manner had a new alertness. He felt that he was coming upon the kind of information that is so often to be found in such cases, and usually constitutes a reliable pointer to those who are responsible for the crime.

"Yes, I reckon it was."

"To whom?"

"That's what *I'd* something to say on. I got him scared when he saw me walk in, and I got the truth out before he'd made up his mind what line of lie to take. I got the benefit of ninety percent of that policy transferred to me three days ago, and the balance goes to the woman that keeps house for him at Chickadee."

"Then if the insurance company pays up, you benefit by his death to an amount of £45,000?"

"Yes. I reckon I do. But he was to sign over to me £3,000 a year out of that salary; which was letting him off light, and I lose that— so I don't do as well as if he'd lived a bit longer."

"Had he undertaken to do this?"

"We'd had it drawn up by a lawyer I'd got working for me, and he was to have come with me to sign it yesterday. When I called then, he put it off till this afternoon, and that's what I came for to-day."

"The document was actually drawn?"

"Yes. It had been sent to him to read over before he came with me to sign. I suppose he's got it now."

"He didn't refuse to sign when you called yesterday?"

"No. He argued a bit, but he gave way. Morrison made him see that he'd get a knock-out in law if he didn't come to terms, now that I'd come over and found him out."

"Morrison?"

"Yes. That's the lawyer I found."

"Bletchworth & Co.?"

"Yes. That's he."

"What time did you see Mr. Bulfwin yesterday?"

"About six in the evening."

"How long did you stay?"

"About half an hour. Maybe more."

"Quarrelling about whether he'd sign this document?"

"Not enough to scare a jack-rabbit. He wanted to make it fifty-fifty, but gave up when he saw it was no go."

"But you must have had a long argument?"

"No. Not more than three minutes. Then he said he'd sign it this afternoon."

"Then why were you in that empty room for more than half an hour?"

"Mr. Starr smiled again.

"Just because we weren't quarrelling, Officer. You can do a lot of that in ten minutes, if you know how. We got talking on how the process would work, and how much the Syndicate might make."

"Talking like that with the man who had murdered your friend, and tried to swindle you?"

"Yes. It meant a lot to us. It was a sure thing that that five thousand wouldn't go on many years, if the process panned out thin."

"He was alone when you left him?"

"Yes."

"In an empty office?"

"There wasn't much there beside himself."

"What did you do when you left him?"

"Dropped in at a show."

"Where?"

"Along Holborn, on the left, going west."

"That was a good way from Fenchurch Street."

"It was the way I wanted to go."

"You say you had no pistol with you at all?"

"Yes. I've said that."

"Where did you spend the night?"

"You've said you don't need to ask me that."

"But I'd rather it came from you."

"Well, it was the Trevor, off Bury Street."

"Thank you, Mr. Starr. I'm much obliged for the information you've given. I shall want to keep in touch with you, and to know where you can be found till the inquest's over."

"Bletchworth's the best address. I shall be there every day, till we've got this thing combed out."

"Could you drop in here tomorrow morning, in case there's anything else you could tell us?"

"Yes. I'll put you wise if I can."

"About eleven?"

"Yes." Mr. Starr went out.

CHAPTER IV.

THE Inspector turned to Sergeant Grover as the door closed, with a brief instruction, causing that intelligent officer to move briskly to the telephone which communicated with the entrance offices. Mr. Starr would be able to observe, if he were sufficiently alert and concerned to do so, that he was not followed. He could not be aware that a very capable plainclothes officer would be in Fetter Lane somewhat earlier than he would be likely to arrive at his lawyers' offices.

"I don't want him to think he's followed, and I reckon he'll make straight for his lawyer when he leaves here. Most men would, and an American first of all—and with all he's got at stake too."

The Inspector said this to the Major, who had now drawn his chair sufficiently near to the table to settle his legs comfortably upon it, and was prepared to exchange theories or observations with his colleague over this unexpected development.

"I think it's he, as like as not, though it's too early to do more than a guess, but I reckon he won't try to bolt, unless he's a good deal more scared than he is now. He's got too much to lose; besides, bolting, with all that's left on the table, would be like pleading guilty at once."

"You think it's he?" said the Major, with an evident doubt.

"I don't go that far. We've a lot to learn yet. I've got Trentham coming back here in half an hour. He'd got a city call he wanted to make, or so he said. Of course, he's followed. But he'll come back, sure enough. We ought to have something rather interesting from him. And Dr. Crowther's report will be here in a few hours. He won't lose any time. And I want to go over the room by ourselves, and we must have a talk with that caretaker, and cook something for the press. You'd better phone that you won't be home till you don't know when."

"Why didn't he want us to know that he'd come over on the *Baltic*?"

"You noticed that? I thought it might only be that he had to think for a second to get the name of the ship. But it was a bit odd. We must find out whether he really did."

CHAPTER V.

THE "voluntary" statement must always remain under the stigma of being radically inequitable. Documents which are the result of questions asked by those who are potentially, if not actually, hostile in judgment, which are reworded by them to their own minds, and which are closed without the explanatory re-examination which a defending solicitor would be entitled to make, must always be under the taint of the process from which they spring.

It is to the lasting dishonour of the judicial bench of our own time that it has accepted these documents with ready hands, until the stifled protests of a thousand prisoners aggregated to an articulate volume which could no longer be condemned or ignored.

But it is probable that this method of collecting evidence has never been less abused than in the hands of Inspector Cleveland, who, being both unimaginative and conscientious, would have admitted a hundred errors of judgment with less mental disturbance than would have been occasioned by the knowledge that he had acted with a deliberate unfairness, or suppressed a fact, for any theory which he had formed, or lest he should be personally discredited by its admission.

Mr. Trentham was an astute man. If a belief which was current at Scotland Yard, and which had caused the Assistant Commissioner to detail Major Cattell-Pratt to investigate his activities, were well-founded, he was a bold and deliberate criminal. But he made no objection to the form in which his narrative was written down, nor to the contribution of his final signature. He was not of the kind who invite direct conflict, though he might be cool and courageous enough if it were forced upon him. His method of warfare was to observe the way which his opponents went, and to dig pitfalls across the path, rather than to meet them with opposition to their advance.

The reader, having the instinctive preference for the straightforward course which distinguishes certain people, will not admire this feature of Mr. Trentham's character. Yet if he were to walk down Oxford Street in a straightforward way, he would receive no compliments from the pedestrians with whom he would certainly collide. Neither will he readily apprehend the symbolism of this illustration, nor will he understand why the Englishman is therefore considered (quite unjustly), by the other nations of Europe, to be of an exceptional hypocrisy.

Mr. Trentham had reason to be satisfied with the careful accuracy with which his answers were recorded, and if he were impatient to return to his Brighton hotel, he allowed no sign of irritation to appear as the slow process continued and sheet after sheet of foolscap was filled up, and laid aside, to be read over and initialled when the examination was ended.

With less formality of detail than the Inspector sought, we may observe that the substance of his evidence was that Mr. Bulfwin had been introduced to him, on his arrival in London, by a City friend, and he had been so impressed with the possibilities of the process which he had for disposal that he had himself put up the capital which had been required in the first instance to purchase the mine, to register the "Syndicate," and to pay the first premium on the insurance policy of which we have heard already.

Having secured these facts, with the dates and details which the Inspector considered essential to his orderly investigations, he went on to ask a few questions which they provoked.

"Even for a financier like yourself," he suggested, with a toneless formality, "was it not rather a large amount to provide single-handed? Rather an unusual procedure to deal with it so entirely yourself, without inviting others to join the risk?"

"Not very unusual in its opening stages, especially when one gets hold of something that looks exceptionally good. But it may not have been wise under all the circumstances at the time."

"Why not?"

"Because I could probably have prevented the failure of the Collman Trust, in which I was heavily interested, had I had the money loose which I had tied up in this way."

This was not a reply which the Inspector had sought and he had a passing wonder as to whether it had been adroitly led up to by Mr. Trentham. He changed his ground of approach.

"Were you aware of any enemies that Mr. Bulfwin had in this country?"

"None whatever."

"Did he ever express fear of anyone, or speak as though his life might be in danger?"

"Never at all."

"Had he mentioned Mr. Starr in any way?"

"Starr?—oh, Kingsley Starr. He always spoke of him as Kingsley. Of course, I knew the name. It was in the deeds of the mine, and the power of attorney which Bulfwin brought. We had to pay half the price of the mine to his order at Denver. He always mentioned him as a pal. He told me that he had come over to England a week or two ago, and that he might want him to meet me. I didn't think he was very pleased about that, but Bulfwin wasn't one to let his feelings show more than he wished."

"I don't suggest that it inculpates you in any way, but it is the fact, is it not, Mr. Trentham, that you gain very much by his death?"

"In a way, yes. I haven't had much time to think it out yet."

"In every way, is it not?—you won't have that big salary to provide, nor any more insurance premiums to pay. You've got the process you wanted for a mere song, at the cost of Bulfwin's life and the Insurance Company's pocket. I don't suggest that you are responsible for his death, as I've said before, but that is how it works out, is it not?"

"I would rather not answer that question."

"You are entitled to refuse to answer anything which would incriminate you."

"I don't follow that. I wasn't thinking of incriminating myself. I thought that if I could see any possible legal complication or disadvantage from Bulfwin's death—and I don't say I do—I should be a fool to have it put down there. But I don't say you're wrong if you say it's a great advantage to me. I can do with a bit of luck of that sort. I've had losses enough."

"Well, I think that's all, Mr. Trentham. Of course, I can get you on the phone, if we should want to ask anything further; and you'll be advised of when the inquest's to be held. You'll be wanted for that...I shall have to get on now. Mr. Pratt's waiting for me in the next room. I'm taking him back to get the evidence right as to how the office came to be opened when it did. Sergeant Grover will read over the sheets with you before they're signed. You must alter anything that's not down just as it should be."

The Inspector, having finished the interview in his more genial manner, went out to join the Major, and the two returned to Bodmin House as rapidly as a police car could make its way through the London traffic.

CHAPTER VI.

"I MADE a point of telling Trentham that you'd be coming back with me," Cleveland said, as soon as they were able to talk in the isolation of the moving vehicle. "So he won't suspect you're connected with us, should he hear it from the caretaker, or anyone else, as he probably may.

"If we're not busy hanging him during the next few months, you might be able to use this murder to get to know him, which ought to help us in lots of ways."

"I don't think I should care to do that," said the Major, rather stiffly. He was often exercised in mind as to the good form of the occupation into which he had drifted. He recognized that it may be the duty of a gentleman to his own caste to weed out bounders among whom certain types of criminals may be classed without undue severity of judgment; but there must be limits to the methods by which this may be done. He was quite willing that his connection with the police should be conceded, so that he might stalk an unsuspecting quarry. He was not prepared to enter into relations of confidence or amity that he might betray the trust he won, even though it might be a dangerous and unscrupulous criminal who would be the victim of his duplicity.

Inspector Cleveland observed the distinction without comment, and accepted the decision without argument.

He said: "I don't suppose we shall find anything of importance. I had a good look round while you were in the next room, but there wasn't much except blood to be seen.

"The man had been shot in the lower part of the body—more than once or twice I should think, and must have walked or crawled about the room afterwards till he died from loss of blood. There were papers in his pockets, and other things that hadn't been disturbed, but they were a sticky mess, and I asked Dr. Crowther to have the clothes cut off as best he could without disturbing them. The only thing I could see that's likely to be any help is a mark that looks like a shoe, and there's not much of that. I told the Sergeant to lay down boards over the floor before the body was moved, and he commandeered some from the basement. We can trust Crowther not to blur any clues. The trouble is that there mayn't be many to blur."

"I don't know that I shall be of much help to you in this," the Major answered. He was seldom disposed to overrate his powers, and he had not been engaged as an expert in the investigation of violent crime. "But it seems to me," he went on, "that it's less than a hundred to one chance that it's the work of anyone from this side. I know I'm set to watch Trentham, and I don't doubt he's a crook. I know that all I've done yet is to think out certificates of character for him, and I'm at the same game again. But I can't help thinking that, if we try to bring him in, we shall be running on a cold scent. The man comes here from the West, and he's been killed in their style. It may be Starr—it's most likely it is—but I think anyway that it's *someone* who's followed him here, or else someone who came from the same parts, and ran against him, with an old grudge to square."

This was loquacity from the Major, such as could only follow from a period of silence, which recent circumstances had thrust upon him.

Inspector Cleveland recognized sense when he heard it, but he had learnt to meet everything in these cases—even the obvious— with an investigating and doubtful mind. Almost always, the obvious explanation was the true one—almost, but not quite.

"You know more of Trentham than I do," he said; "is he British or States?"

"English," answered the Major, "born in Ipswich."

He gave details of ancestry and collaterals, showing the patient thoroughness with which he had familiarized himself with his subject. A great-uncle on his mother's side had been transported for forgery: a Quaker ancestor of his paternal grandmother had lost his ears for a religious "libel": a distant cousin was now suffering imprisonment for the theft of a motorcycle, an occupation in which he specialized.

Covering, as it did, the lives of several hundred people, it was negatively a good record, as the Inspector saw.

"What line was his father?"

"He kept the Sandringham Hotel. The son went into a stockbroker's office till he was twenty-three, and left that to take on the hotel management when his father died. It was while he was doing that that he met young Ratspate, who used to put up at the hotel when he was too drunk to go home. He used the knowledge he'd got in the stockbroker's office to swindle him out of about £5,000 in such a way that nothing could be done without a scandal that Lord Roughton wouldn't have faced for ten times the amount.

"After that he sold the hotel, and came to London. He set up as a stock jobber, and then started one thing after another that took in a good deal of other people's money, and didn't pay much out, but we haven't found anything definite enough to act on yet, as you know."

"Well," said Cleveland, "it isn't a family record with much bloodshed about it. You may be right. Here we are."

CHAPTER VII.

THERE was not much to be gained from the room, as Inspector Cleveland had feared. There were a pen and a full three-penny bottle of black ink on the window-sill. The room had no furniture, except the blood-stained linoleum, on which some planks had been laid crossways, so that it was possible to make an examination without treading upon the floor.

"There was nothing to help us just round the body. I made sure of that before I agreed with Crowther to have it moved to the mortuary. It's this side I didn't want trodden over. What do you make of this?"

The Inspector pointed to a blood-mark which was about a yard from the left-hand wall—the farthest stain on that side. At the edge which was nearest to the wall, it was slightly broken by three short parallel lines.

"Not much," said the Major, truthfully. "What do you?"

"Rubber-soled shoes are not very commonly worn, but such a mark might be caused by one: Kingsley Starr wears that kind of shoe."

The Major looked sceptical. The marks were short, and not very distinct.

"It's a bit thin, isn't it?" he said doubtfully. "Honestly, Cleveland, would you have thought of it, if you hadn't noticed the kind of shoes that Starr wears?"

He thought that the Inspector, having observed Mr. Starr's peculiar footgear, had searched the floor with a determination to find something to correspond. Well, if this were all the result, it wasn't much.

"I hadn't noticed Starr's feet when I spotted these marks. I looked at his feet and Trentham's afterwards to see who could have made them. Trentham couldn't."

The Major was impressed. It was true that this information did not increase the size or significance of the marks, but he recognized that it did increase the probability that the Inspector had read them accurately.

"You don't miss much," he said, with an increased respect for the patient thoroughness of his companion's methods, which were so like his own, though he did not use them to equal ends.

"There's not much to miss here, worse luck." He was cutting out a large patch of the linoleum as he spoke. "They can clean up here tomorrow. There's no more for us. I'll have Mr. Lytton Kingsley Starr's shoe measured with this mark, and if it fits, we'll have him arrested before he gets out of bed. You'd better go out before me, Major, if you don't mind. It's no use trying to dodge the Press. If you tell them how you came to look into the office, and keep Trentham and Starr out of it as much as possible, you can't do any harm. It may do good. You can tell them that the case is in the hands of Inspector Cleveland, and that the police have got a clue. It often makes the criminal act the goat when he reads that. And give them plenty of blood. The public likes blood."

The Major walked down the silent passage, and looked at his watch. It was eight o'clock. He rang the lift-bell for the caretaker to let him out. Doubtless, Cleveland would be here for another hour questioning that flustered individual. A whimsical idea that he might be the unsuspected criminal entered his mind, and bolted quickly when it realized the common-sense contempt which received it.

The Major did not want to interview reporters. He wanted a good meal in his own flat. But for the hint he had received, he would have stubbornly declined to discuss the subject. But he would do what he had been asked, though not to the detriment of a waiting meal.

At a time of leisure, and with sufficient deliberation, the Major liked a joke. That is, he liked one of his own, which he knew to be of a finer substance than was commonly recognized by others.

When the lift stopped at the street level, he gave one of his cards to the caretaker, asking him to phone Miss Cattell-Pratt that he would be home in half an hour, and be ready for a good dinner. He gave him a shilling.

He got out half a dozen other cards, on the backs of which he wrote, "Doors open at 10:00 P.M."

So armed, and smiling at the rich humour of this endorsement, he allowed the caretaker to let him out and distributed them to the eager press-men that were round the door.

CHAPTER VIII.

As Major Cattell-Pratt inserted his latch-key in the Yale lock of his quiet and comfortable flat, with a pleasant anticipation of the waiting meal, he heard his sister's voice at the telephone.

"Well, of course, if it's an appointment," she was saying, "but you can't come at ten. Mr. Barrington's coming then. Very well, if you really— Yes, but you mustn't come at once. 9:15."

"Hold on, Cora—I say—" began her indignant brother. But the receiver was already back on its hook.

"I don't know whether you've gone quite mad," she remarked, as she led the way to the dining-room. "But that's the sixth ring I've had in the last twenty minutes, and every man says that you've made an appointment at ten o'clock, and wants to see you alone, and before anyone else does. I've done the best I could to spread them out."

"I won't see anyone till I've had dinner, and a good rest after that. I've done enough for today. I didn't promise to see anyone alone."

"You've got forty minutes before Mr. Atkins comes—that's the one I've spoken to last. There'll be one every ten minutes then, and two at ten. No one would agree to be later. It's Mary's night out; so you can talk to them while I wash up."

The Major said nothing to that. He sat down to a leg of lamb with green peas and mint-sauce, of which he was fond, and his temper steadied itself under the pleasant influences of the hour.

He was soon being questioned skilfully upon the events of the afternoon, and, under the stimulating influence of the mint-sauce, and having a well-founded confidence in his sister's discretion, he narrated his somewhat startling experiences with a fullness which cannot be commended to other officers of the Criminal Investigation Department when they are interrogated by their lady relatives, as they too often are.

"I'm rather surprised at Mr. Cleveland," Cora remarked, as she considered the final episode of the afternoon. "I rather liked him when you brought him here last Christmas."

"Yes," said the Major, with brotherly candour. "Everyone saw that."

"I expect they did. It wasn't the three children; it was the red-haired wife that was the real obstacle."

"What's her hair got to—? I wish you wouldn't talk rot. Anyway, what's he done now?"

"I don't see why he'd got to nose about for those shoe-marks. It might make no end of trouble if they fit Mr. Starr's shoes, as I suppose they will."

"Then you think he did it?"

"It sounds that way, doesn't it?"

"Yes. I think it does. Trentham had as much motive. Rather more to gain, though not so much to resent. But I don't see how we can connect it with him. Not so far, anyway. There may be more to come out. But you can see it's a good thing you've kept clear of Trentham."

"Yes?" said Cora. She looked puzzled. "Perhaps it is. What are you going to say to Mr Atkins? He's due in about ten minutes. I expect that's his ring. It ought to mean a new dress for the summer."

The Major looked puzzled in his turn, and his sister was quick to pass him the fruit-dish.

"Have an orange," she said sweetly. "There's no reason why they should interfere with you till you've finished dinner. He's come too soon. I'll tell him he's got to wait."

She went very cheerfully to the door.

The Major heard a murmur of voices for a few minutes, and then the door closed, and she came back.

"I think I'll have one myself," she remarked, as she resumed her place. "There ought to be time before the next one's due."

"How did you get rid of him?"

"I didn't. He's coming back. Mr. Atkins represents the United Press. I told him that you couldn't honourably give an exclusive interview before ten, as you'd said that the doors opened at that hour. He's gone away to phone his office, so that he'll know what to quote."

"What to quote?"

"Yes. You didn't mean to do it for nothing, did you?"

"Look here, Cora, you're going a bit too fast. You mustn't forget I'm on the staff. And I can't tell them all I've told you. You'll get me into trouble over this, if you don't take care. Anyway, I can't make it exclusive to one paper—"

"It wouldn't be that. You know the United Press would give it out to about fifty. I don't know whether it goes to all the papers that will buy it, or if they have their own ring. You ought to know about that."

It didn't happen quite as Cora had meant it should, and some information had to be given to reporters who had no connection with the United Press, but she had a cheque for thirty guineas from that wealthy organization a few days later, and, as she remarked to herself, it might have been worse. It gave her an increasingly friendly feeling for Mr. Kingsley Starr, whom she regarded as the originator of this very profitable excitement.

CHAPTER IX.

MAJOR CATTELL-PRATT of the C.I.D. (you *must* be careful about the Cattell, putting at least a couple of hundredweight of accent on the last syllable—his mother was a Cattell of the Slushford branch) had had an uncomfortable half-hour that morning with the Assistant Commissioner.

Not that he had been rude, or unreasonable, or even unsympathetic; nor did he make the mistake of calling him Cattle-Pratt, as was too lamentably frequent among his brother officers at the Yard. It was just because he *was* being reasonable that it had been so hard to endure.

"You know," he had said, rising from his chair, and walking up and down the room in the stress of an irritation to which he did not allow a verbal exit, "It isn't as though I'd asked you to do impossible things. I don't say you must catch a fraudulent financier once a fortnight. You did well in the Lidworth case. We both know that. We mention it every time you come here to report. If you don't, I do; and if I don't, you do. But that's two years old now.

"I don't want to rub it in, but you can't go on for ever on the strength of that one success. It isn't as though you'd come in at the front door, so to speak. Of course, there's the unemployed officer— 'wounded in the war'—argument, that got you here, first, as a kind of extra. That's all right. And it meant that you ought to have a chance, and so you had, and you did well. I'll always say that.

"You showed you'd got nerve, and it looked as though you'd got brain; and so I gave you this Mortimer Trentham to follow up— and that's nearly two years ago."

He had thrown a half-smoked cigarette into the grate, and lighted another immediately.

The signs had been ominous, for he was a man of controlled speech and actions, and had caused Major Cattell-Pratt to speculate somewhat anxiously as to the probable conclusion of the interview.

And he had had nothing to say. He had reported failure, which is soon done. There was no more—or, at least, not much more—to be said; and what there was must be kept in hand for a last extremity.

So the Assistant Commissioner had gone on.

"It isn't as though the man *might* be straight. If I thought that, I'd call you off, and say it had been my mistake from the first. But we *know* he's a crook. We *know* what happened over that Ipswich matter, only Lord Roughton couldn't be persuaded to prosecute. And then the Albemarle suicide. And now there have been two more promotions, and two more smashes, and you and your City friends watching him all the time, and he just walks off, and you tell me that there's nothing that you can get at—and he doesn't seem to have made a penny from first to last. Is it sense?

"And so I suppose he'll be quiet again for six months or twelve, and then start a new game.

"And now, Major, just tell me this. I know it's hard on you, and I know how you're placed—but can I call you off this man, and just say you've failed, and then put you on to something else that our regular men might handle better, and couldn't handle worse; or can I keep you on, just to wait and watch for another chance at the man, that may end in the same way?"

"No, sir; I don't see how you could. But I don't think it means much waiting this time. There's something on foot now, though I can't tell what yet. He's taken an office off Fenchurch Street—just a single room, with a good address. It's not taken in his name, but he's the only one who's been there and there's some sign-writing ordered. That'll show something."

"Already? That isn't his usual way. I thought you told me that he was finishing off with the typist at Brighton, as he always does?"

"So he is, to a point. He's got her there, and he's spending money as freely as ever. But he's coming up to London two or three times a week. I was going to ask you to have him watched. I know it's proved useless before, but I've got a feeling that it might be different this time."

The Assistant Commissioner had sat down. He had made a note.

"Go ahead," he had replied, with a resumed geniality. "I'll see that he's watched well. Cleveland can take that on, with any help that he needs, and report to you as often as you wish. You can get him on the phone, and he'll only come to you if there's an urgent need. It's not wise for you to be coming here too often. Don't think too much of what I've said. I expect you'll haul in the line at the finish."

He had shaken hands quite warmly. He meant it to be Major Cattell-Pratt's last chance, but he knew that men do not do their best work when under a cloud.

CHAPTER X.

THE press-men had gone at last, and the Major, drawing quietly at his pipe, had sunk into one of his usual silences. Cora saw that, if she were to obtain any further information upon the day's events, she must exert herself to that end.

"You didn't tell me you were calling at the Yard today."

"I don't quite follow."

"You're not likely to find out anything worth detecting if you can't follow that."

"Well, then, I haven't. So you thought wrong."

"Haven't what?"

"You'd be no good at detection if you can't follow that. I mean I have been to the Yard, but I didn't get sacked, as you thought I should."

"Ted, I am glad! I hope they gave you something better to do."

"No, they didn't. Niblett gave me a last chance to catch Mortimer."

"That was before they knew about this murder?"

"Yes. I'm not put on to that. It's about his financial operations. It doesn't follow that he's involved in the murder at all. I don't suppose he is."

"Then I'm afraid it isn't much of a chance. I don't mean it's your fault, but he's too wary. Anyway, you should have let me help before now."

"It's no use asking that, Cora; I've told you twenty times that it's not work for girls. I hate it myself, but I couldn't get anything else."

"You're not likely to do much good, with that feeling."

"I did well enough in the Lidworth case."

"Yes. And you were fresh then. New broom and all that. I've always said you should let me help."

"I'd never do that."

"Anyway, you can tell me what you think he's getting up to this time."

"There's not much to tell yet. I only know he's just taken that office, and they've painted up the new name—this Bulfwin, who's got shot."

"You can't make much out of that."

"No. I can only watch. But this murder will probably blue it, whatever it was."

"How did you find out?"

"Through Billy Trickett. He knows I'm interested in Trentham, and of course most people are talking about him in the City just now, so he mentioned he'd seen him go in at Bodmin House. Then I saw him there myself yesterday, so I thought I'd inquire for an office this afternoon, and see if there was anything I could pick up."

"Suppose you'd met him?"

"It didn't seem likely; and it wouldn't have mattered if I had. He didn't know me at all. Of course, we did meet, the way things happened, but it wasn't so that he could think that I was taking any interest in him.

"Anyway, if he were up to another game, I wanted to watch from the start."

"Perhaps he isn't. Hasn't he always had an interval between his enterprises? I thought he retired to Brighton with a typist. Is it always the same?"

"So he does. No—different.

"He's had a confidential lady secretary each time, who's stood by him during the smash, and been rewarded at last. I suppose he knows how to pick them. The weekend type of young woman, but one who looks as though she'd have some loyalty and a share of brains."

"You seem to know. Look here, Ted, there's only one chance for you, and that means for me too, unless I'm to end life as a char-lady. *I've got to get that job.* By the way, what becomes of them, when they leave the seaside? If you hunted up the discarded typists, you might strike oil there."

"So I might, but it can't be done. He left one of them in Paris, or she left him. 'Gone, no address' now. Another wrote to a friend that she was off to Los Angeles, and was changing her name to something more suitable for a film star. It was something like Shufflebottom, so you can't blame her for that. Jane, I think. But she didn't say what she was changing it to, and that was the last of her. Number three's with him now. Or, at least, was. He said something about a secretary having been drowned at Brighton this morning."

"Well, if she weren't, she'd better clear. Number four's on the doorstep. I'm glad I had that six months at Purford's Practical, though it didn't lead to anything better than an offer of fifteen shillings a week, and find your own soap, towel, boot-leather, tea, and travelling expenses out of that, which I gave up, as you know, because it didn't seem fair to put you to so much expense. What's the shorthand for contango? Is it a 'G' or a 'J'?"

"I wish you wouldn't talk such rot. You know you couldn't get the job, and I shouldn't let you if you could."

"Ted;" his sister answered, in her sweetest tone, but setting a small mouth mutinously, "you've got to drop that. I was twenty-one yesterday."

"I don't care if you were eighty. I'm fifteen years older than you, and I'm not going to let you get into any mischief like that. But, oh, I say, I didn't mean to forget. I really didn't. Are you sure it was yesterday?"

"Not from memory. It's hearsay evidence, really. Though I suppose I was present at the time. Authority of tradition more than anything else. But you needn't worry. I bought myself a new hat, and told them to send you the bill, so you didn't really forget. Not to matter, anyway. But, Ted, if you're a beast about this, you'll be sorry for a good while. It will simply mean that I shan't take the job in my own name. Not Cattell-Pratt, nor Cattle-Pratt. And I shouldn't take a new name altogether, because I might forget it myself.

"'Will you kindly take down this letter, Miss—er—I'm afraid I forget.'

"'Very sorry, Mr. Mortimer Trentham, it's the same here.'

"I might call myself Prattle-Cat. That's near enough to the truth, and it isn't the sort that anyone forgets before they need to use it again."

The Major pushed his chair back sulkily. Cora knew that he knew that she knew that he hated jokes about the honourable name they shared, and she ought to know better than to make them.

It wasn't that he hated *all* jokes. We know that he liked to make one now and then himself. But he liked his jokes to be deliberate, isolated, well-rounded, and of a seemly subject. Cora went on chattering, and you often couldn't tell whether she were joking or not, and before you could think it out properly she might have made two more.

Still, she was a very charming girl. She was a Cattell-Pratt. What more need be said?

He was going out of the room, when she added, "I'll come with you tomorrow, Ted, to look at the new office you're supposed to be taking, and you can introduce me to Mr. Trentham, if he's on the spot. It'll feel like making a start."

"That you won't," he said with decision; and then, changing his mind, "Oh yes, you shall, if you like. The man may be there, and I'll see you come under his notice in a way that'll make him too suspicious to engage you afterwards."

"Perhaps you're right, Ted," she answered, meekly. "I don't think I will."

She had no change of intention, but had decided that she could play this game best by herself.

He was content with the victory of the moment, and subsided into his habitual silence.

CHAPTER XI.

MR. (OR MAJOR) CATTELL-PRATT sat in a low chair by the November fire for a full hour after he had risen from the breakfast of eggs and bacon which is the portion of all right-thinking English-men. He ate that breakfast as he performed all his national duties, and those of the social order to which he belonged. Had he ever been guilty of such bad form as to thank Heaven for his own virtues, he would no doubt have expressed his gratitude to a Power which had not made him a crank. It would not have occurred to him to thank Heaven that he was not a snob, though he would have repudi-ated the suggestion with genuine indignation and partial truth.

He might have been puzzled to define what he meant by a crank, but it was really a comprehensive word, covering all support-ers of minorities of an aggressive or unpopular kind.

A man who had declined to wear stiff cuffs with a soft shirt, when those detached linen ornaments were popular, would have been a crank. A man who wore them today would be a crank, and might deserve to be described as a bounder also, which is depth be-low depth.

An anti-vivisectionist was a crank. But should opposition to vivisection suddenly spread, so that it would become a general atti-tude, he would cease to be a crank, without necessity for any change in himself, and would become a respectable member of the commu-nity.

The Major's reading was from *The Times* and the *Morning Post*. He studied the financial columns with a somewhat slow but retentive mind.

He rose at last, and went to the telephone. He got through to Mr. William Trickett.

"That you, Bill? I want you to buy me a hundred Cobbetts at not more than five and seven-eighths. If they fall more today, you can make it two. No, it isn't a safe tip. It isn't a tip at all. I just thought I'd like a few, if they're cheap."

He put back the receiver, and went to a davenport in the far corner, where he took out a diary and made careful note of the order which he had given.

He was not the first man to find a treasure which he had not sought. He had taken to a daily study of financial news, that he might be the more able to comprehend the wiles of his appointed antagonist, and in the course of two slow-thinking years, he had gained so firm a grasp of the movements of the financial markets that his cautious and limited transactions were the index by which other operators were guided in Mr. Trickett's office, to an extent which he would have found it hard to believe, and with results which added greatly to that gentleman's reputation for sound advice, and augmented his business accordingly.

It may be thought that these successful transactions should have gone far to render him independent of the very moderate salary which he received for his services to the civil power, but the fact was that he would as little have thought of appropriating any of his stock-exchange winnings to the expenses of the flat, as he would have thought of risking his small capital upon the currents of that treacherous sea.

His speculations had commenced vicariously, when he had made an astute suggestion to Mr. Trickett, which had resulted in Bill and his friends, with a decisive boldness which would have appalled the Major, netting something over £5,000 of which he had accepted, with some hesitant protest, a ten-percent commission, which had been the nucleus of his subsequent operations.

No fascination of quick profits, no allurement of margins, had ever tempted him to risk anything beyond the sum which lay in the separate account which he had opened for these transactions, and though his capital had now grown to over £4,000, he would have regarded any suggestion of withdrawing a portion of it for the mere pleasure of spending as a chess-player, using pieces of precious metal, might do if he were asked to surrender one of them in the middle of a game, so that it might be realized in the melting-pot.

The telephone rang.

"That you, Major? Yes, Cleveland. I didn't mean to ring up so soon, but we've learnt something that you may like to know, though it may have no direct bearing on anything that you have on hand. You know Trentham'd got his secretary with him at Brighton at the Palatine? Well, she was drowned yesterday morning. Boating accident, quite early. No, I don't see how he could. He was in bed at the time. There's no doubt of that. Still, I thought you might like to know. Yes, of course. We shall overhaul her things, if we get half a chance. I've got a man at the hotel now, seeing what he can learn. No, a collision. Half a dozen in the water. Other boats near, and they were soon fetched out, but Miss Neilson was dead. No thanks; not another call. That's all now."

The voice ceased, and the Major went thoughtfully back to his chair. No, he didn't think that the young lady had been murdered. He wasn't a romantic ass. Mortimer Trentham was *in bed*. Surely that was enough.

Still, they *did* disappear, one way or other. That was a fact. He turned it over thoughtfully in a slow mind.

Finally, he was overcome by the temptation to show the wisdom of his prohibition of the night before. He shouted, "Cora!" and that young lady came from the kitchen, with flour whitened hands.

"Well," she said, "what have you lost now?"

"I haven't lost anything. I haven't wanted anything that you've moved yet, though I expect I soon shall. But I've just had the details of something that it may do you good to know. I shan't ever learn anything from number three. She was drowned at Brighton this morning. You can see the sort of trouble you might get into, if I weren't here to look after you."

"I suppose you mean that he drowned her?"

"No, I can't say that. He was in bed. But it isn't healthy to be one of his secretaries, it seems to me."

"Well, anyway, it was better than having to be a film star."

She went back to the kitchen.

The Major felt the satisfaction which is experienced by the male who has displayed his wisdom, like a peacock's tail, to an admiring member of the more foolish sex, but he would have been less at peace had he been able to observe the smile that parted two mutinous lips, as the knife ran quickly around the pie-dish edges. But Mortimer Trentham might not be so easy to trim.

CHAPTER XII.

SIR HARRY NIBLETT, Assistant Commissioner in the Metropolitan area, held a conference in his own office. There were two of the chief officers of the C.I.D., in addition to Inspector Cleveland, Dr. Crowther, and Major Cattell-Pratt, who were immediately concerned with the case, and the sole question to be determined was whether he should order the instant arrest of Lytton Kingsley Starr for the wilful murder of Mr. Bulfwin, or inform the Coroner that the police were not prepared to act, in which case an inquest must be held.

"So far as Trentham is concerned, there is really nothing to connect him with it, beyond the fact that he stood to benefit by the death. We couldn't arrest him on that. Can we go further, and rule him out in our own minds? What do you say, Major? You know more about him than anyone else."

"Well, sir, I don't think it's he, and I don't see how it could be. I can't go further than that. I've got the feeling that Trentham plans out his deals from the start, and if he'd *known* that the man would be murdered just when he was, he couldn't have done better for his own profit. That way, it looks just like something he might have planned, but there's not a shade of evidence that he did, and we've found out that he was certainly in Brighton during the previous forty-eight hours. Then there's no record of violence against him. As far as I know, he's never fired a shot in his life, even at a rat or a rabbit."

"What do you say to that, Cleveland?"

"I can't say the Major's wrong, sir. We've accounted for every hour of Trentham's time at Brighton, and we can't find that he had anyone with him that could have come to London during the time. There's his secretary being drowned the next morning. Of course, that's a queer thing, but it appears to have been an accident. There's nothing to go upon against Trentham at all."

"Very well. Rule him out. Now we come to Starr. I've read his account. He admits that he had good cause for quarrelling, and, as far as we know, he was the last one to see him alive. How do his statements come out, so far as you've been able to check them?"

"I haven't found anything wrong. It's true that he went into the Empire that evening. A programme-seller remembers him. He's a man that might easily be noticed. Of course, that doesn't show he didn't do it. On his own account, it's most likely he did, but I can't get the bit of extra evidence that I need, and now Dr. Crowther's queered the pitch in a new way."

"We'll come to that in a minute. Let's finish with Starr first. I understand that he didn't go back to the Trevor last night?"

"No, sir; and he didn't want to give us that address at all. But there's something queer about that too, and I can't make out what it means. He'd left the Trevor that morning, and paid his bill. He didn't mean to go back. He took a suitcase away in his hand. That was all the luggage he had. Of course, that looks as though he'd done it, and was preparing to hide. But, if so, why did he go back to Bulfwin's office? There's not much hiding about that. Then what followed is queerer still. I sent a man to watch outside his lawyers' in Fetter Lane, and he went there, just as we expected, and stayed for about an hour.

"When he came out, our man followed him along the Strand, and over Waterloo Bridge He says he went straight on, but didn't hurry, or try any tricks to get away, and when our man turned the corner of Cobden Street, he'd stopped, and was waiting for him there. He made some remark about it being more sociable to walk together, and they went to private hotel—the Ellam's—about half a mile farther on."

"Making the best of a bad job?"

"Our man doesn't think so. He says he got the idea before then that he was *anxious* to be followed, and afraid of being lost if he went too fast. But that isn't all. He took the man upstairs to his room, and told him he could look at anything he liked He'd got a pistol packed at the bottom of his grip. He said he hadn't had it out since he left Chickadee. It didn't look as though it had been used."

"Bullets fit?"

"No, they wouldn't. That's in his favour, but, like the rest, it proves nothing. He may have had two, and thrown the other away. It's the same with the shoes. I'm certain that we've got the mark of a rubber sole, of the kind he wears, but the shoes he's wearing now don't quite fit."

"No mark of blood on them?"

"Not the least. But again that doesn't disprove anything. He may have had two pairs, and thrown one away. The other queer thing's this: he hadn't moved into Ellam's yesterday. He'd been there all along."

"Had he been sleeping at the Trevor?"

"Yes, so they say, and they seem to think he had at Ellam's too, but they're not so sure. They gave him a latch-key there, and he went in and out as he liked. There's another hotel, a larger one, under the same management, the other side of the road, and most of the staff sleeps there, so there isn't over-much supervision, not that that point's of any importance, as far as we can see yet."

"But it looks as though he had prepared to hide himself at any time by having these two addresses?"

"Yes. It does. But, if so, why didn't he try to hide when he'd shot his man?"

"He must have altered his mind, or his nerve went, as it often does."

The Inspector shook his head with a scepticism only restrained by the respect which Assistant Commissioners inspire.

"No, sir; he hasn't lost his nerve. But I don't say we couldn't bring it home but for what Dr. Crowther says, and that doesn't show it wasn't he, it only shows we've got more to find out before we've finished this case."

"Well, Doctor, we'd better have your report now."

Dr. Crowther spoke with deliberation. He had the type of mind which is careful in deduction and exact in statement. If he were somewhat oracular in manner, it was a not unnatural result of the deference which his opinions had earned—a reward of many years of precision and impartiality.

"The cause of death," he said, "was hæmorrhage from four bullet wounds in the abdominal regions, none of which could have been self-inflicted. The first two were fired at the same time from almost opposite directions, and from distances of two or three yards, more rather than less, while the man was standing. The third and fourth shots were almost certainly fired after he had fallen forward. He probably lived from ten minutes to half an hour after receiving the first two bullets. The bullets were of slightly different patterns—two of each. That is, in brief summary, the evidence from the post-mortem examination."

"Can you say how long he had been dead?" the Assistant Commissioner asked.

"About twenty-four hours, more or less. It would be impossible to tell to a few hours. It was certainly not much longer. Probably less."

"When you say he was shot from two directions, do you intend to imply that he must have been shot by two people at the same time?"

"Yes. That is quite certain."

"It could not have been done by one man, having a pistol in each hand?"

"No. It would be impossible owing to the distance from which the shots were fired."

"I don't quite see, Doctor, how you can say with certainty that two shots were fired at the same instant."

"It would be impossible but for one circumstance. The two bullets collided, and continued their course side by side, each having been somewhat deflected by the other, though in unequal degrees."

"Well," said Sir Harry, "that seems final. I understand that there was no indication that the contents of the pockets had been disturbed. Do they help you, Cleveland?"

"Well, sir, I think they may. Anyhow, they're rather interesting. There was the agreement for assigning part of his salary to Mr. Starr in his breast-pocket, and that was higher than the other papers, and rather crooked, as though someone had pulled it out, or half out, to see what it was, and then pushed it back till it got caught on another. There are two sets of fingerprints on the deed. I thought I'd struck oil when we found them. They're small, and Starr has a small hand, but they don't appear to be his."

"Tried Trentham's?"

"Not yet, sir; but it's hardly worth doing. His hand's about twice the size."

"Does the agreement confirm Starr's tale?"

"Yes. Everything does that we can check. It's what we can't that floors us here."

"Were the other papers of importance?"

"There's one that may be, though it's hard to say how. It's a letter from a Soviet Commissioner, and it seems to show that Bulfwin was trying to double-cross Trentham, as well as Starr, if he could get enough to make it worth his while."

"Anything else?"

"There were some receipted bills, and a wallet of notes, and some private letters that don't seem to lead anywhere, though there's one or two things in them that we're following up on the chance. There were some keys and oddments in the lower pockets, and some loose money. But we can't find the office key, which he must have had. Of course, whoever killed him would have needed that to lock the door when he left. But there's one thing certain: they couldn't have got it out of the lower pockets after he was dead without getting themselves in a mess, and leaving traces of what they had done. In fact, we're certain the trouser-pockets had not been disturbed."

"He wasn't armed?"

"No. But the shape of his hip-pocket showed that he usually carried a pistol. We thought we might find it at his hotel, but it isn't there. Of course, he may not have brought it to England."

Superintendent Withers spoke for the first time. He was a mild-mannered man, who looked as though he might cross the road to avoid a sheep, if it wore horns, but he had a reputation for some of the coolest and most sensational arrests and intricate crime-solutions of his time.

He said, "Is the process really valuable?"

"I can't answer that," said the Inspector. "Everyone seems to think it is. That seems clear enough."

"I think, sir," said the Superintendent, turning to Sir Harry, "that's the most important question of all, if we're looking first for the motive. If Starr or Trentham—or both of them—knew it was a fake, there was only one sure way of closing down with a good profit, and that was the insurance."

"I don't quite see that," said the Major. "Trentham might have floated it for a good sum, and then let it smash, as he's done before."

"He might have meant to do that," Withers answered, "and then altered his mind when he saw how things went with the Collman Trust. He may have thought it too dangerous, and changed his methods; but it's no use guessing on these points till we've got the first question answered. Is the process genuine? Is it the sort of thing that could be patented? And, if so, has anything been done on those lines? And if not, why not?"

"I haven't missed that," the Inspector answered. "I asked Trentham, and I've got his explanation in his statement. He said he didn't want to patent unless he were obliged, or not till the last moment anyway, because there's a lot of platinum mined in Russia, and it would be giving it away to them. He said he had opened negotiations with the Soviet Government to sell to them for a cash sum, but he couldn't get them to decide. That seems reasonable enough, and it's borne out by the fact that Bulfwin was trying the same game."

"Then you think it's a genuine discovery? Can you tell us anything of its nature, or what they claim that it does?"

"I don't know more than what Trentham explained, and what I've looked up since, and I mayn't put it quite right, but I understand that platinum is never found pure. It's mixed up in the ore with iridium and other alloys, and it's not easy to separate them. That may be because platinum isn't easy to melt, but I don't really know.

"Anyhow, platinum ore isn't easy to refine, and this process is said to do it at about a third of the present cost. I can't say whether it's really any good, but I think they all believe it is."

"I don't want to criticize, Cleveland," Superintendent Withers went on, "I think you've handled this thing really well. I can't see that you've missed anything, and you've been prompt every time. And I think there's something due to the major too. If he hadn't been following Trentham up as close as he was, we shouldn't have come on this in the way we did. And it's easy to get slack when you've been on a cold scent for nearly two years."

The inspector allowed a little smile of satisfaction to appear at this praise—from such a quarter it was high praise, indeed—but the Major's face was impassive, although it meant more to him, and was unexpected, for he had only been conscious of the exasperating fact that he was unable, as usual, to do more than demonstrate the improbability of Trentham having any connection with the crime. But they may both have waited with some interest, if not anxiety, for any sting which might lurk in the tail of the Superintendent's remarks.

He went on, "I'm not criticizing, as I've said, but if we allow the process to be genuine, I still think there's one point on which you should concentrate. We can take it, I think, that it was a carefully planned crime (there's one point I don't understand, though the explanation may be quite simple. I'll come back to that), but when we're dealing with a crime of that kind I always look first for anything that *couldn't* have been foreseen, and what influence that may have had.

"Now, you've got a hand-print, and, perhaps, a boot-mark, that you can't place, and if you succeed with them you'll probably be able to pull in the line with a full catch; but, meanwhile, there are only two men you can suspect at all—Trentham and Starr—and you get them both coming up to that office in the afternoon, almost at the same minute, with the dead man the other side of the door. Now they couldn't have known that the Major would have got that office open a few minutes before they came. Whatever they did expect, it wasn't *that*.

"If they were innocent men, of course they were just ordinary calls. But if we go on a theory that one or both of them knew what was the other side of the door, then we have to ask what course of action had they planned to take? I'd give something to know whether either of them had the office key in his pocket."

"Trentham had a duplicate key," said the Inspector. "He told us that."

"Then you ought to find out whether they had two from the landlords, or where they got it made. If he's told a lie about that, and he's got Bulfwin's key in his pocket, it's just the sort of little thing that might hang him, if he were asked suddenly in the witness-box for an explanation that he couldn't give."

"But I've checked on that," the Inspector answered. "He had it made at Hinton's, in Lion Court."

The Superintendent looked mildly disappointed. "That scraps one idea," he said frankly. "I thought it possible that Starr might have asked him to meet him there, knowing that he couldn't get in if he arrived first, perhaps having Bulfwin's key himself, or perhaps meaning that they should have to go to the caretaker when they found Bulfwin wasn't there to let them in. That was on the supposition that Starr had done it, and wanted to look innocent by being there when it was found. But, of course, he mayn't have known of Trentham's key. I still think those two men coming up as they did holds the explanation to everything, if we could only work it out. But the other thing that's puzzled me is the caretaker's part in the matter. Why didn't he hear the shots? Of course, they may have used silencers, if it were a planned thing. And why didn't he find it out sooner? Most caretakers open their rooms once a day."

"There are one or two of these points that do seem a bit queer," the Inspector answered. "But not so much as you think before you look into them.

"As to the last, the tenancy didn't really commence till today— June 25th—though they'd signed the lease, and got possession, nor did the caretaker begin to get anything for cleaning the room till to-day, when the furniture was to come in. Trentham's put it off till tomorrow now, to get it wiped up, and some new floor-covering laid down. Then as to the noise. Billings—that's the caretaker's name— lives in the basement, but there are some alterations going on there, and he's been sleeping with his family in rooms a couple of streets away for the last fortnight. The rule is that he closes the street-door at six-thirty, but will let any of the tenants in if they ring. They can open the door from the inside, if they stay later, and are supposed to pull it shut, which he says they don't always trouble to do. While he's been away at night, he's been fastening the front door open till eight-thirty, and then going round the building to make sure that no one's left inside, before he double-locks for the night and goes home.

"As to anyone else hearing, if there were no one left in the offices near, the street traffic might drown it, even if ordinary pistols were used without silencers. Some of them aren't very loud. But there's another point that comes in here. We mustn't think that it need have happened between six and seven in the evening, because we suspect Starr. It might have happened any time during the night, and while these repairs were going on in the basement, it wouldn't have been very hard for anyone who'd let himself be locked in to get away. There's a yard-wall about eight feet high, and nothing worse than that till you're in a passage to Mortmain Street. Of course, it isn't likely that Bulfwin would have waited in an empty office after closing hours for someone to murder him, but there's the fact that, if they had done it then, they could have got clear.

"No one saw anyone leaving under suspicious circumstances, so far as we've inquired yet, and I've had two good men doing nothing else. And so, there we are."

"Well, gentlemen," said Sir Harry. "Is it to be an arrest, or shall we let the Coroner get to work? You haven't spoken yet, Gilkes; what do you say?"

Superintendent Gilkes lifted heavy eyelids from delusively sleepy eyes to answer, or rather ask:

"Anyone see Starr leave? Was he alone?"

"There's only one man who says he saw him, and he says he left alone," the Inspector answered. "But we can't trust what he says. He says Starr left at eight o'clock. He's sure of the time, because he had just closed his shop—he's a tobacconist opposite—and was going for the eight-eleven at Fenchurch Street, which he caught, when he saw him come out (so he says), and pull the street-door shut after him. The trouble about that is that Starr was in the Holborn Empire about half an hour before that, if another witness is to be believed, and I think she's the better one of the two. Anyway, they spoil each other. It's the usual thing."

No one quarrelled with that statement. Many of a detective's troubles would disappear if he could eliminate the inaccurate individual who, from love of notoriety, or excess of imagination, pushes in to confuse the evidence with assertions, confidently made, which must be patiently probed, with loss of time and temper, and sometimes worse consequences if he be too readily credited.

"I should say it was Starr," Gilkes said, "all the same. If you arrest him now, you'll probably have all the evidence you need before it goes into court."

"Then you advise his arrest?" the Assistant Commissioner asked, doubtfully.

"No, I wouldn't say that. There's a risk."

"It would be better if we could go on a coroner's warrant?"

"You won't do that, sir," he answered. "Russia. You'll see."

With this cryptic utterance, Superintendent Gilkes's eyelids descended to their previous level.

"You'd better tell the Coroner he can go ahead," said Sir Harry, with decision, and the conference ended.

CHAPTER XIII.

THE inquest on the enterprising but unfortunate Bulfwin was not a long one.

The jury went through the rather useless formality of "viewing the body," or rather the face of the deceased, a ceremony which is at the Coroner's discretion, and which has been very generally omitted in recent years, during which three closed their eyes, five gave a fleeting glance, under compulsion of their oaths, and to the detriment of their dreams, and four would willingly have looked somewhat longer but for the pressure of the moving group at their rear.

They were not asked to inspect the wounds which had occasioned this investigation—which would have been somewhat difficult after the surgical explorations which had preceded them—and it is not easy to see what advantage could result from this ceremony, unless it were to demonstrate that there really was a dead man in the case, and that the whole entertainment had not been staged for the weekend reading of the nation, by a patriotic Press, or a paternal government.

They moved obediently in a single file beside the sheeted figure, and returned to their places to hear the evidence of Mr. Billings and Major Cattell-Pratt as to the discovery of the body, and that of Dr. Crowther as to the nature of the wounds it bore.

It was only in reference to the doctor's theory of the two first shots being simultaneous that there were any questions asked, but Mr. Dibber (instructed by Bletchworth & Co.), who appeared on Mr. Starr's behalf, was rather curious on this point, and led the doctor to give a very exact and detailed description of the courses of the two bullets until (he said) they had encountered one another, and both had been deflected, continuing almost side by side, until the leading one had stopped when actually touching, but without injuring, the spinal column.

"Though," the doctor added, "it is possible that there may have been sufficient shock to produce a temporary paralysis of the lower limbs, causing the immediate collapse, which appears to have occurred, the course of the other two bullets, Which were fired at a closer range, indicated that the man was either lying face downwards, or on his hands and knees when he received them."

"It appears," said the Coroner at this stage, "that the deceased was a citizen of the United States, and his passport shows that he was on a business visit to this country. We have at present only succeeded in tracing two gentlemen with whom he had any intimate business or personal acquaintance, one of whom is said to have been with him alone on the evening before, and in the office in which his body was found. Neither of these gentlemen is obliged to give evidence, should he consider that it might tend to incriminate himself, but their legal advisers are present, and I am informed that they both desire to give us such assistance as they are able to do."

Mr. Trentham was then called. It would be tedious to set down his evidence, so far as it repeated that which he had asserted before, and which remained unchallenged. A man cannot be accused of complicity in a murder which takes place fifty or a hundred miles away simply because he benefits financially by the event.

There was only one point on which he was cross-examined at all, and that was by Mr. Starr's solicitor, who commenced in a way from which few could have guessed the point to which he was leading.

"Since the discovery of platinum," he began, "I think I am correct in saying that the bulk of the mineral has been obtained from the Russian mines?"

"Yes."

"Over ninety percent?"

"Possibly. The Russian figures have always been unreliable."

"Understated, rather than over?"

"Probably."

"Then there could be little importance in this process, unless it were adopted by the Soviet Government?"

"That does not follow at all. Its greatest value lies in the fact that it would make many deposits commercially valuable, which it has not been possible to work hitherto."

"Then," said Mr. Dibber, speaking with an increased deliberation and emphasis, "is it not true that this process is not only of great potential value to the Russian Government for their own use, but that it would be of enormous importance to them if they could obtain, or even suppress it, because of its probable effect, not merely in reducing costs, but in opening new sources of supply which must restrict the demand for the Russian product?"

"Yes."

"And the Soviet Government has been approached?"

"Yes."

"They knew what was claimed for the process, and that Mr. Bulfwin was, or had been, the custodian of the formula?"

"Yes."

"And the office where he lost his life had been taken for the marketing of this process?"

"Yes."

"That is all, thank you," said Mr. Dibber, and sat down. Mr. Trentham left the box.

Mr. Starr gave his evidence confidently. He admitted his differences with the dead man, and the extent to which he might gain by his death. He repeated in substance the account of their final interview which he had given to Inspector Cleveland. He was unshaken in any serious particular, though the Coroner questioned him somewhat severely.

He accounted for his two hotels by saying that after he came to London, and put up at one, he had got lost—he was not used to cities of such a size—and had been obliged to find accommodation elsewhere, being unable to remember the address to which he should have returned. It was two or three days before he found his way back to the first hotel, and he had then decided to keep a room at both, so that he could return to whichever should be nearer, after the nightly wanderings in which he indulged. It was, at least, a possible explanation.

He made a good impression on the jury, excepting only that two or three were disposed to doubt whether he could be a genuine American, as he lacked the strength of accent, and the wealth of idiomatic speech to which they were accustomed by the talking films. Fortunately for his credit with these people, he had replied, "That's fine," when told that he had given all the evidence which the Court required.

The Coroner summed up briefly and fairly. He thought the jury would have little difficulty in deciding that this was a case of murder—brutal murder of an unarmed and defenceless man. So far, he did not see that any other verdict was possible. But to decide where the responsibility lay was a more anxious and difficult question. A suggestion had been made—it would be a poor compliment to their intelligence to suppose that they had not understood it—that the murder might be the work of the emissaries of a Great Power with whom we were at peace, if not in actual friendship. He must tell them that there was not an atom of evidence to support such a suggestion, which, he felt, should not have been made. It came from the solicitor of one—Mr. Kingsley Starr—who was not himself free from the shadow of suspicion. He appeared to have been the last man who was known to have seen Mr. Bulfwin alive. He had a grievance—if his evidence were to be believed, a great and genuine grievance—which was being adjusted only under legal pressure; and such an adjustment could hardly produce any feeling of goodwill. It was not a voluntary restitution. They might think that a grave suspicion rested upon Mr. Kingsley Starr. But suspicion was not proof. They must not forget that Dr. Crowther had said definitely that the murder could not have been the work of one man. If they felt that they could do no more than to ascribe the homicide to some person or persons unknown, they could rest assured that the matter would not end there. It would become the duty of the police to continue such investigations as would in all probability result in such persons being brought to justice at last.

After this summing-up, and with Mr. Dibber's hint firmly planted in the minds of the jury, there could be little doubt as to what the verdict would be. They found that Mr. Bulfwin was murdered, but there was not sufficient evidence to say who were responsible for the crime.

CHAPTER XIV.

INSPECTOR CLEVELAND laid a set of photographs on the table. "I'm up against it here," he said, "and if you can't help me, I don't know who can."

Superintendent Withers said quietly, "Let's see what the trouble is."

The Superintendent was not a man of excitable disposition. When a desperate criminal had confronted him with the muzzle of a six-shooter, and announced that if he were not out of the door in ten seconds it would commence exploding in his direction, he had only answered mildly, "I don't think I should, if I were you. Haven't you got a chair where I could sit down?" He had an air of rather weary patience with the follies of the criminal population. No one had ever known him to hurry, but neither had they known him to stop, and the amount of work he got through in the year must have been very great. Inspector Cleveland came to him for consultation not only because he was the recognized expert on fingerprints at the Yard, but because he could be relied upon to listen patiently to any statement, however improbable, and to approach its solution in a leisurely level-headed way which was often very consoling at times of unusual worry or indecision.

The Inspector spread out the photographs as they were numbered from one to six.

"The first four," he said, "are from the deed which was in Bulfwin's pocket when he was shot. The fifth is the thumb of Kingsley Starr's right hand, and the last one is his right hand complete. These first two show the marks that were at the top of the document, back and front."

The Superintendent picked up the first two photographs. The one showed the front of the top joint of a thumb. That was a very clear print. The other showed the side of a finger. It was not equally well defined, but sufficiently so to be readily recognizable. They had been taken from each side of the top of the deed.

The next two photographs were larger. One showed the side of a thumb, down to the ball. The other showed four fingers more or less completely. They had been taken from the opposite side of the same document, lower down.

When he had looked at them, he picked up those which had been obtained from the right hand of Kingsley Starr. He looked at the thumb first and said, "You can't go beyond that. It's a different hand. It rules Starr out, so far as that it shows another man was there. But Crowther's always said there were two."

Cleveland made no answer to that, for he saw, even as the words were spoken, that the Superintendent's eyes were upon the sixth print. Let it speak for itself.

It was evidently doing that. Superintendent Withers was looking at it with an intentness which had forgotten his own words, and was in no expectation of reply. He examined the other prints again. He got out a microscope, concentrating upon the junction of the first and second fingers in the fourth print. There was a long silence. He laid down the microscope, and sat thinking silently. Then he said, "You know this is absurd?"

"Yes. That's why I've brought them to you. I know it's impossible. And yet there it is."

"You can't say it's impossible. Ever heard of the card deals that come out one complete suit to each player?"

"Yes. But I don't believe them."

"No. You're probably right. But they're not impossible. It's only millions to one that they're not true. It's countless millions to one here. Indeed, it's that multiplied by itself, as you've probably seen if you've thought it out. Any theory?"

"None about that. I'm just beaten."

"Apart from that. How and when do you reckon the marks came on the deed?"

"That seems simple enough. The man who shot him must have pulled, or half-pulled, it out of his pocket, and then tried to push it back. It didn't go far back, if at all, because it caught in the top of a shorter paper—a letter—and the man didn't trouble any further. But for that, I suppose the lower marks would have been more or less rubbed off.

"I reckon the man pulled it out with his hand on the side, and then loosed it, and tried to push it back, holding it at the top. We've got to remember that Bulfwin was lying on his face, and the man would feel what he was doing, rather than see."

"Any idea why he changed his mind?"

"Nothing certain. He might have been looking for something else, and pushed it back when he found it wasn't what he required. Or he may have taken something that he *did* want, and this came partly out with it. Or he may really have been uncertain whether it were best to leave it, and changed his mind. It's mere guessing beyond that."

"Yes. Suppose it were Starr? It would be best to leave it, wouldn't it? Much."

"Yes."

"And it was left. Of course, it may have been pulled out completely, and then put back. Both men may have handled it."

"Yes. But the positions of the marks. And the fingers join."

"Yes. Those are the real difficulties. But you know there always *is* an explanation. Quite a simple one, more often than not. It's like a chess problem that you haven't solved. When you've been at it for a couple of hours, you're quite sure there's a misprint, and when you've worked it out, you wonder you didn't see it at the first glance."

Inspector Cleveland thought misprint was rather a good word, but he saw no consolation in that.

CHAPTER XV.

"TED, there's a telegram for you on the davenport," Cora remarked, as they got up from dinner about a week after the date of the abortive inquest.

"Is there?" he replied without enthusiasm. "Then why didn't you tell me before?"

"Well, it's been there since midday, without being any trouble, so I thought it might go on waiting while you had something to eat. You know I never fuss."

"Well, I don't suppose it matters. It's probably only Bill worrying about the drop in Associated Plasters. He's always wanting me to sell on a bad market. I suppose that's how brokers live. *Oh, I say, Cora, I'll never forgive you, if—*" He pulled himself up from the momentary excitement which the telegram had aroused, and became his restrained and dignified self again as he passed her the buff slip, with the remark:

"I suppose Saturday's done that. I hardly know whether I ought to accept. Baird must have been rather desperate when he thought of me."

"Of course you'll accept. You know that as well as I do. We'd better get a wire off at once."

She picked up the reply-paid form which the envelope contained.

"It's no use spoiling that. It wouldn't get through tonight now. I might get Baird at his club," her brother interposed; any excitement he might feel being insufficient to disturb the common-sense coolness with which he usually faced an emergency.

"I'll see if he's there now."

She went to the telephone, and rang up the Gardiner.

"Is Mr. Baird in? Yes, T. A., of course. Please find him, if you can; it's important." And then, after a surprisingly short interval, "That you, Tommy? This is Cora...Cora Pratt, of course. Who did you think? Ted's only just had your wire. Yes, he'll be there. And about time too. I think it gets stodgier every week."

"You might have let me have a word with him."

"I didn't know there was anything more to say. You can ring him up again, if you like. You didn't want to *thank* him, did you? When they've been playing duds like Thorne and Joe Mackintosh."

The Major said no more.

He was one of those unfortunate cricketers who are always on the outskirts of county rank, but who fail to gain a regular place in the team. He had played more than once or twice, and was known as an attractive hard-driving bat when he got going. But he was without subtlety. He was not strong in back-play. He had no reverence for the two-eyed stance. He went for all bowling more or less in the same way.

He had made many high scores in weekend games, and a hard-hit 136 not out the previous Saturday, on a pitch which most of his team found too difficult for their comfort, was doubtless responsible for the present invitation from the Middlesex captain.

Tomorrow was Wednesday, Cora reflected, when the match would commence, and, if the skies were reasonably clear, there would be few things more certain than that her brother would be at Lord's from noon to six-thirty, and for the same periods, more or less, on the two following days. She could have no better opportunity. She reflected that the dispensations of Providence may be underrated by thoughtless or flippant minds.

CHAPTER XVI.

IT WAS three o'clock on the following afternoon when Cora entered the Kensington High Street station, and took a ticket for Mark Lane. She had dressed herself with unusual care, aiming to combine an effect of business efficiency with as much feminine charm as could be consistent therewith, and being fortified with the new hat which her brother had so thoughtfully provided.

Arriving at Bodmin House, she learnt from Billings, who was in charge of the lift, and whom she easily recognized from her brother's description, that she was fortunate enough to have called when Mr. Trentham was in the office.

She stood a moment outside the door, not from any hesitation of nervousness, but because a lively imagination enjoyed the thought of the sign writer inscribing BULWIN'S SYNDICATE, LIMITED upon it, in ignorance of the sight which lay upon the other side, awaiting those who should be the first to open it.

Then she knocked, and a voice of dignified geniality invited her to enter.

Cora had the feminine characteristic of swift and detailed observation. A well-educated and cultured woman may never be able to recollect more than a few of the leading facts of the history of her own land, such as that Mussolini won the battle of Hastings and that Harold was killed during the following century by an arrow in the eye, shot by Wat Tyler, when they were hunting together at Senlac, in the New Forest; but she will be able to memorize the physical characteristics and clothes of half a dozen women in the same number of seconds, and to make an approximately accurate guess at where the various articles were purchased, and how much eleven pence, three farthings a yard the materials cost of such as were not ready-made at the time of purchase.

Cora observed a rather large room, furnished *en suite* in light oak and dark green leather, having an air of ease rather than affluence, or of an affluence that would not boast.

Mr. Trentham sat at a large flat desk in the centre of the room. There was a high pile of letters before him, which he had been commencing to open. Clearly he had only arrived a short time before her.

There was a table against the opposite wall, with a new typewriter shining upon it, and a neat array of inkwells and pads, and wicker baskets and other office requisites.

She saw with satisfaction that they had an almost aggressive virginity, and this appearance, with the absence of any feminine occupant of the room, led her to conclude that Mr. Baird's invitation had not been issued too late for her purpose.

She had not seen Mr. Trentham previously, and was surprised that he was not more formidable or sinister.

These things (and many others) she observed as she took three steps into the room, the while he rose, and paid gratifying tribute to her own appearance by the courtesy of tone and manner with which he placed a chair, and inquired her business.

We have the authority of Lord Tennyson, who professed to admire them, for the opinion that even the best of women are skilful, if not habitual, liars. I can offer no other excuse for the easy mendacity of Cora's reply.

"I hope you'll excuse me calling without an appointment, but I am looking out for a secretarial position, and my brother—Major Cattell-Pratt—suggested that you might have a vacancy here. I don't think you really know him, but he was at the inquest on that horrible man who got killed here. I expect you'll remember. He was looking over some offices at the time."

"Yes," said Mr. Trentham. "Y-es. Oh yes, I remember." He was disposed to add, "Rather a fool, isn't he?" but realized that the query might be ill-addressed to his present auditor.

Seeing that he was in no haste to reply further, Cora went on:

"I'm afraid I can't give you any very good business references, but I've had a full secretarial training—Purford's Practical. Of course, I can do typewriting and shorthand. My speeds are ninety-seven and—"

Mr. Trentham interrupted her, with a smile which, she thought critically, improved an expression which was normally too near to pomposity.

"It's no use telling me those, Miss Pratt. They never mean anything. Besides, I don't know what they ought to be. I know one has to be a good deal more than the other, but I never remember which."

"I'm not sure that I do myself, without thinking, but I thought it was the proper thing to say," she replied, with an answering smile.

Mr. Trentham observed the dimple in her left cheek with some approval. His glance passed to a chin that was small and firm and rather deeply divided. Certainly a pretty chin. And her lips were admirable. Like most men, he could admire pretty lips best when they were unpainted.

Looking somewhat higher, he met her eyes, and became conscious of the interval of silence.

"Yes, Miss Pratt?" he said, as though he had been waiting for her to continue.

His thought was that she would make a very attractive secretary. It would save time and trouble, too, not to have to wade through the pile of letters before him, which were in reply to an advertisement which he had inserted three days ago. It was curious that this call should have come so opportunely. Still, the explanation was natural enough.

With that light fluffy hair, and the blue eyes in the small face, that dimpled to laughter so easily, she had an almost childish expression. But attractive. Very.

If he could be sure that she had the brains, and the character—the particular kind of character—which he required. Not for the Syndicate. Any good quality secretary would do for this—but for the further plan, to which this was only an interlude He became aware that she had been talking for some moments, and that he had not heard what she said.

"—when I left, and I think they would, but, of course, it wasn't very long."

"No," he said vaguely. "Not very. But expect they would, as you say."

Cora wondered, was he only waiting for the moment when he could show her to the door without impoliteness? Surely he could not be nervous—or shy?

He said, rather abruptly, "What salary were you having?"

"I thought of asking four guineas," she replied indirectly. She had considered while in the train that if she did not value herself no one else would. She had decided to ask three guineas then. It must have been the new hat which gave her confidence to plunge for the additional unit. It had been a rather expensive one. It would have been wrong to undervalue the generosity of a brother's affection.

"Week or month?" Mr. Trentham inquired.

"Four guineas a week," she replied, with enough change of tone to indicate that she did not approve the query.

"Was that what you have been having?"

"I had a little less than four guineas."

"Well, I don't think we should quarrel about that."

He considered that that tone and manner might be invaluable under some possible future circumstances,

He said, "You had better let me have your address and that of the reference you gave. I'll let you know in a day or two. I expect we can fix it up."

She drew out a card, writing the other address on the back. She thought she had won, but was not as certain as she had intended to be. She looked at the farther table with a proprietary feeling, as though it were already her right, which he delayed.

It may have been this feeling which prompted her to prolong the conversation. The murder that the room had seen so short a time before had been in the background of her mind all the time. "Out of the fullness of the heart the mouth speaketh."

She said, "I couldn't help rather liking that Mr. Starr, though I suppose he did it, more likely than not. But I was glad the shoe didn't fit."

She knew her folly, as the words left her lips, and as she saw the startled query that lit for a moment, and was then hidden behind his eyes.

"Shoe?" he said. "I don't think I heard of that. It sounds interesting."

She realized that she had betrayed both herself and her brother's confidence, but she saw also that the only chance now was to speak with an apparent openness and simplicity.

"Hadn't you heard?" she said. "Ted—that's my brother—heard the police talking. They thought they found the mark of a boot in the room, and they tried whether it would fit Mr. Starr, and were quite disappointed that it didn't. At least, that's what he told me he overheard. Of course, I may have got it wrong. I expect you know more about it than I do."

She paused, feeling that she had said enough, and conscious of a possibility of misconstruction in her last words. But Mr. Trentham did not appear to notice them.

He only said, "You didn't tell me when you could start."

"I'm free any time you wish."

"Then suppose you begin tomorrow morning. I'm coming in then, to meet Mr. Starr. You'll be working under him more than me. At first, anyway. I don't think we'll trouble about the reference. They never mean much. Say eleven. Then we can go into matters properly, and you can have the key, and come earlier after that."

CHAPTER XVII.

CORA bought an *Evening Standard* as she entered Mark Lane Station, and turned first, as most people do in the summer months, to the cricket news, in which she had, as we know, a particular interest.

The report of the Middlesex match had a sub-heading, *Cattell-Pratt Batting Well*, on seeing which her eyes went eagerly to the smaller type, to read:

> After a rather shaky opening, Major Cattell-Pratt appeared to get the measure of the bowling, and drove with power on both sides of the wicket. He narrowly escaped being stumped on one occasion when he stepped out to Pritchard and missed the ball, but he took eleven off that bowler's next over, a three to the off being followed by two straight drives to the screen....

Cora turned hurriedly to the stop-press news to read:

> Middlesex—268 for 8
> Cattell-Pratt—79 not out

She decided that the Cattell-Pratts were having a good day.

She was home in time to superintend the preparations for the evening meal before her brother came in, and received her congratulations with a satisfaction chastened by the fact that he had failed by three runs to reach the coveted century. He had been 97 not out, and every cricketer knows that to be even 99 not out is a very inferior thing to having your wicket spread-eagled when you have made a hundred In a laudable anxiety to give the Major the bowling, the last batsman had run himself out.

Cora would not admit that she was nervous—fancy being nervous of Ted!—but the first course was over, and she had brought in the macaroni and cheese, before she found courage to say:

"It's been rather a good day for both of us."

"Yes?" said the Major, without excitement.

"I've got a job at four guineas a week."

He looked really startled at that. Pleased, perhaps; but incredulity was also indicated.

Finding that she was in no hurry to say more, a slight irritation supervened.

"I suppose it's one of your jokes," he said doubtfully. "You wouldn't keep it at that, if you had. I wish you'd say straight out what you mean."

Cora's courage returned with the knowledge that she had burnt her boats, and must give unavoidable battle.

"I mean that I've seen Mr. Trentham this afternoon at Bodmin House, and he's engaged me as his secretary, or for the Bulfwin Syndicate—I'm not sure which—at four guineas a week, beginning tomorrow."

She saw the angry protest on her brother's face, and went on quickly, "It's no use looking tragic. He isn't at all what you think. A child could manage him. Besides, I needn't keep on, if I don't want to."

"You know what's happened to the others."

"No, I don't. Neither do you."

"You know one of them's drowned."

"Well, whose fault was that? You don't really suppose he drowned her, do you? Anyway, it's only thirty-three and a third percent."

"It isn't a joke. I shall write and cancel it tonight."

"I don't think you will—and it won't make any difference if you do, because I shall be waiting there when Mr. Trentham arrives if you do, and it's a secretary's duty to open the letters. I'll tell him I can't swim if you like, and then he'll have the sell of his life when he gets home from the dreadful deed, and finds I arrived ten minutes earlier, and am just changing into dry clothes."

It was Cora's general experience that when she was flippant on a serious subject Ted kept his temper with difficulty, and when he lost it, he was very likely to lose the argument also. But he was too much in earnest, and too genuinely alarmed on this occasion, to regard the manner of her retort.

"It isn't only the risk," he said seriously, "though I don't trust them an inch, either him or Starr—they're both in it together now, and it looks as though it'll blow over. The Insurance people told us yesterday that they don't see anything to do but to pay. It isn't only the risk, but it isn't work that's fit for a girl. You know you're only taking it as a spy. I told Cleveland that I wouldn't do that sort of thing myself, though I am on the staff, more or less."

"Of course you wouldn't. I should never speak to you again if you did."

"Then it's worse for you."

"No, it isn't the same at all."

"I don't know what you mean."

"I mean I'm not on any staff. I can do as I like."

"I say you're only going to spy, and if you're doing that...."

"But I'm not going to spy for you. I'm going to spy for myself. I just want to find out. When I know, I'll decide what to do. I mayn't tell you a thing. I may fall in love with him, and go off to Brighton, like the rest.

"Look here, Ted," she continued, changing to a more serious tone, "you must see there's a difference. If you took a job with him like that, you'd be *bound* to use it against him, whatever you found out, or if he told you in confidence. But I'm not in that position, and I don't feel like that at all. It doesn't follow that if I found out that Starr did it, that I should let the police know. I should be quite as likely to hide his shoes. But, oh, Ted, I am sorry. It just slipped out. You know it isn't like me to do it. I told Mr. Trentham about that."

"About what? You surely didn't mention that I...."

"I didn't do any harm at all. At least, I don't think I did. I got out of it well enough. But I know it might have been different."

"You haven't said what you did tell him yet."

"Yes, I have. I told him about the shoe that didn't fit."

"Then you've let him know—"

"No, I haven't. I said you overheard the police talking about it. Anyway, he engaged me after that."

And then, as she said it, a doubt came into her mind. He had certainly engaged her after that. Just after. Had he engaged her *because* of that? It seemed unlikely, but it was a possibility she could not entirely exclude.

The Major was silent. She thought him magnanimous, as, indeed, he was. But he was also thoughtful. He had an idea, such as she must have spoken at once, but he was content to turn it over quietly, and examine it on every side. In the end, he decided that it was sound. He saw that, had it been a calculated indiscretion, it could not have been better chosen.

"He wouldn't think from that that we had anything to do with the police. He'd think that you wouldn't have mentioned it, if so. It must have made him feel you were quite safe; but there won't be much chance of finding the right shoe now—not if Trentham had anything to do with it."

For the moment, he seemed to have forgotten his opposition, or, perhaps, he realized that he could not restrain her at this stage of her projected folly. She took advantage of the pause to produce a very creditable yawn.

"I think I'll go to bed now, Ted," she remarked, in the sleepiest voice that she could contrive, being particularly wide-awake at the moment. "Mary can clear in the morning. We both need a good night's sleep."

"Mary?" he said: "I thought it was Mary last week."

"So it was," she replied, in a voice which had forgotten its part, in the stress of indignation which that joke always produced. "She's been here nearly two months."

"She must be hiding from the police."

"Good night, Ted."

Cora had the discretion to sacrifice the pleasure of the last word for the success of her strategic move to the rear. She went promptly to bed.

CHAPTER XVIII.

CORA found Mr. Trentham awaiting her appearance on Thursday morning, but Mr. Starr did not arrive till a few minutes later.

The two men greeted each other with a polite formality, from which she immediately concluded that they had not been associated in the murder of Bulfwin, or any previous enterprise. It might not be a legal proof, but it was a sound and, to her mind, a certain deduction. She thought, also, that there was an instinctive antagonism between them.

Mr. Trentham introduced her politely.

"This is our new secretary, Mr. Starr: Miss Cattell-Pratt. You'll remember that her brother was present when the—when Bulfwin was found."

Mr. Starr looked a second's surprise at the connection, which may have been natural enough. "She thought his expression was alertly defensive as he turned toward her. Their eyes met, and she was aware of an instant lifting of the hard veil of his, to disclose something more frank and friendly than she had expected to encounter. Hands met, and she was aware of a very muscular grip, from fingers scarcely larger than her own. They did not hurt, but she had a feeling that they might have done so very easily.

The man gave her the impression of a lithe and perhaps predatory personality, but one that might be very pleasant when it purred. He was like a—no, not quite like a leopard. Not so restless. Was it a panther she meant? Or a puma? She wasn't quite clear between the two. She thought one was rather thicker than the other. He wasn't thick. But the puma was an American animal. And a nice word. Puma it should be. She was aware that Mr. Trentham was speaking again

"Miss Cattell-Pratt can tell you something about that murder, Kingsley, if you're still interested. She knows more about it than we—than I do. Her brother's heard the police talking. They've got a clue, or a shoe, or a shoe that's a clue, or it may be a shoe that isn't. Miss Pratt knows, anyhow."

Cora thought that he must have composed that sentence beforehand. Mr. Starr looked at him with expressionless but wary eyes. Cora felt that the puma was not far from a spring. Yet the feeling was born of instinct only. He gave no sign. If he sprang, it would be without any previous warning. Not even the sinuously-moving tail which is the way of his kind.

She had an impression also that Mr. Trentham was well aware of the feeling which he provoked. That he did it carelessly, if not deliberately. He was the larger man of the two. Physically, he rather attracted her. Like most women who are not tall, she had an instinctive preference for larger men. But she was aware that he had no thought or reliance on physical advantage. He was not a man of his hands, or a user of lethal weapons. Ted had been right in that. Rather, he was like a man who goes unarmed into a wild beast's cage, and finds it sport to test how far he can tease, and escape alive. She saw that he had courage enough of his own kind—but it was the puma for her.

All this was of a moment's thought or feeling—a moment of silence, following Mr. Trentham's announcement, and then Starr said:

"I've got an automobile, but I can't get used to this right-hand drive. Could you steer it for me, Miss Pratt?"

Evidently, he did not intend to discuss clues.

"Yes, I can drive," she said. "Is the car here?"

"It's not far away."

Mr. Trentham interposed. "I didn't know you were wanting a chauffeuse, Kingsley. I engaged Miss Cattell-Pratt for our work here."

"I guess that won't take all her time, if you did," was the indifferent answer.

He went on, "I've had some of that cash you sent to Denver cabled back, so I've got a few dollars in hand, and Morrison tells me he'll get the insurance money before the week's over, so if Miss Pratt'll run me around, I'll buy a house somewhere. They tell me they're not to rent in these parts."

"Do you want to get out of London, Mr. Starr?"

"I want to get somewhere where I've got room to move, and where the sky shows."

"Then you're settling down in this country?"

"That's too big a slice to cut. I'm here for a time, and I'll have somewhere to live. I suppose I can sell, if I quit."

Mortimer Trentham interposed again. "Suppose we talk business first, and you can fix up for Miss Pratt to drive you round afterwards, if you want to. You'll find a Minute Book on your desk, Miss Pratt. If you'll take notes of anything we decide, you can enter it up, and we'll both sign before we leave. That's always best, when there are only two on the board. You won't find it hard to follow, because you know all about our business already. Everyone does, since that cursed murder. I've agreed to Mr. Starr coming on the board in Mr. Bulfwin's place, and to some revision of the terms of purchase, and we're here this morning to get these things fixed up, and to settle details. That right, Kingsley?"

"Yes. That's the star turn today."

During the next hour, Cora kept her mouth shut, and her pencil busy. At the end of that time she had increased her knowledge of both men, and somewhat reversed her previous opinions.

Of Mortimer Trentham's business capacity there could be no doubt. The minutes which he finally dictated to her, in which, as governing director, and in accordance with powers conferred upon him in the Articles of Association, after allotting shares and dealing with other routine business, he added Mr. Starr to the board, and then set out the conditions of his appointment and remuneration, and the revised terms for the purchase of the process which it was their purpose to exploit, were models of brevity and precision. But, as a bargainer, he had hardly shown the expected qualities. He had certainly accepted proposals which were less favourable to the company, and therefore to himself, than the original agreement with Mr. Bulfwin—terms, indeed, which went far to neutralize the financial advantage which he had gained by Bulfwin's violent end, with its consequent termination of the salary and insurance premium liabilities which he had undertaken.

The explanation might be no other than that he feared the legal position which would result should Mr. Starr attempt to repudiate the sale which Bulfwin had made on his behalf. Cora was unable to assess this possibility; but she observed that Mr. Trentham seemed more concerned to get the terms clearly set out, beyond risk of future misunderstanding, than to improve them to his own advantage.

Mr. Starr, on his side, having a fixed idea as to what would be fair, did not attempt to go beyond it, and, as the discussion proceeded, he appeared to recognize that his protagonist was only using his superior knowledge of English business and legal methods and phraseology for the service of their common purpose, and to modify his own tone and. manner accordingly.

When she had entered the Minute Book, Mr. Trentham read it aloud.

"I think, Kingsley," he said, "that's got it about right."

"Yes, that's great," was the cordial answer, and the two men signed.

She thought that the discussion had brought them nearer together than they had been previously.

At the end, they agreed to meet again in a week's time, when their new agreements would have been put into legal form, and it was probable that there might be some advance in the negotiations which had been reopened with the Soviet Government, which Mr. Starr left in the hands of his colleague in the meantime.

Cora was given the keys of the office, and of a substantial safe, and some correspondence to sort and file. The formula and the more important papers of the company were in the hands of the Porchester Safe Deposit Co., and it was agreed that it would be best to leave them in that custody.

"There's nothing much else to do, except entering up the Share Register till we meet again," Mr. Trentham said, as they rose to go, "so there's no reason you shouldn't drive Mr. Kingsley (Cora wondered whether he always got that gentleman's name wrong by error or design) round the country for a few days, if he's anxious to go, but he wouldn't find anything better for a single man than a flat near Hyde Park, or a good hotel."

"I shan't want you to drive me that long, Miss Pratt. I want to buy a place straight off, and be in it on Sunday. We've got all the afternoon; and tomorrow to settle up, if the agent isn't on the spot today."

"You won't buy a house like that in England, Mr. Starr."

"Well, I reckon we can pay a deposit tomorrow, and move in Saturday, and settle up next week. I shan't have the cash before then."

"What price do you want to pay?"

"I don't mind fifteen or twenty thousand if it looks good. Dollars, not pounds."

"Then they'll want about a month before they'll let you get over the doorstep. The more you pay for a house, the longer it takes to buy it. Isn't that so, Mr. Trentham?"

"They won't do it for anyone under three or four weeks, Mr. Kingsley. Miss Pratt's right there."

"Well," said the American, "we'll see about that. We'll get busy looking round, anyhow. You'd better come and have some lunch with me somewhere, Miss Pratt, and then we shan't get lost."

Cora thought the same. She was much more inclined for a run through the Surrey hills than for the writing up of the Share Register, as to the nature of which she was not nearly as clear as a student of Purford's Practical should reasonably be expected to be. They went out together.

CHAPTER XIX.

CORA decided that Mr. Starr had no manners, either bad or good. He might not be likely to push in front of her through a door, but she was sure that he would do it without hesitation should he feel disposed, and that he would feel contemptuous should anyone consider the incident seriously. But he was not naturally inconsiderate. Evidently not to one whom he had taken under his care.

He led the way at a rapid pace to the nearest restaurant, without consulting her wishes, but he was abruptly urgent that she should order the meal to her own liking, afterwards confining his own requirements to a glass of water, and so lean a meatless meal that he might have been requested to leave, had not the waiter thought fit to veil his contempt, in consideration of her more substantial appetite.

She had not finished her soup before he brought up the question of Mr. Bulfwin's decease with a disconcerting directness.

"I guess you Britishers think it was a rotten way Bulfwin got crocked."

"I don't know what most people think. I shouldn't say that he was much loss to the world."

"I reckon he only got what he asked for. If you—" He checked abruptly. "I might tell you more some day," he said, in rather lame conclusion. Cora finished her soup without looking up, and in an outward calmness. But she felt that the puma's eyes were upon her, and she guessed his thoughts with some accuracy. She was as conscious of the admiration of his glance as though she were looking directly at him. She thought, with a delightful thrill, that if he were not in love with her already, he ought to be so before sunset, if she managed at all properly. She thought he looked at her as a puma might look at a doubtful but tempting piece of meat in his path. It seemed innocent enough, and was juicy beyond doubt—if he could be *quite* sure that there was no cunning trap concealed. He had been indiscreet already—almost.

She wondered what he might think or do—if he should learn that her brother held an appointment with the C.I.D.

The waiter changed her plates, and he spoke again, his mind evidently still on the same subject.

"Ever shot anyone up? Can you use a gun?"

She met his eyes at that, and the dimple showed in her left cheek as she answered, "No, Mr. Starr, I can't say I have. I suppose you plug someone out West more days than not. Plug is the right word, isn't it?"

Mr. Starr's admiration was unconcealed. "Dames like you don't need to shoot," he said, and the inference, though obscure, was evidently of a complimentary character. "But you'd be safer in that office if you'd got a gun in the drawer. No, we don't get quite as busy as that. It might be a better place to live in if we did a bit more, now and then. You'd find it'd save something in jails here. But I don't carry a gun in this country. I never got my gun out till the officer fished it from the bottom of my grip. Never once."

That seemed definite enough, and she felt that he was telling the truth, even though the purpose of his previous remarks might have been to lead up to that declaration.

"I suppose you felt it was polite to fall into our ways," she said, showing him the dimple again. "Like using chopsticks in China. I hope you didn't find it quite as difficult to do."

"Well, I'm not losing weight," he said easily, "not to notice. I've not got overmuch to lose, but I'm feeling fine. I say, where are you going to take us this afternoon?"

Cora felt some difficulty in deciding that. The country within thirty miles of London, which was his limit, must include about 3,600 square miles, which is a considerable area to commence to examine when it is already 2:15 P.M. She asked for some indications of the type of house and surroundings that he preferred. She spoke of the wooded beauties of Kent and Surrey hills, of Chiltern hollows, and Berkshire downs, and of the green loveliness of the Thames.

"I don't know about *hills*," he said sceptically. "Anything seems to be a hill here, if you can't see over the top without standing on a bench. But we've got to begin somewhere. Let's try the first that you said."

"Very well. That was Kent. We'll run out towards Sevenoaks. There's some lovely country that way, and it's not too far. Perhaps we'd better go to an agent first, and get some particulars."

But Mr. Starr would not hear of that. He appeared to have some bitter memories of the vendors of "real estate" in his own land.

"We'll find what we want first," he said definitely, "and then we'll get it the best way we can."

So they made their way to the car which he had garaged in a side-street, a last-year's second-hand Morris-Cowley two-seater.

"Not one to pick for her looks," as he said truthfully, "but light and quick, and a good engine, and I've had them clap on some new tyres."

They ran out clear of the London suburbs, and were in the neighbourhood of Orpington, when he said, "This'll do, if you can get us clear of the crowd."

They went by side-roads after that, Cora slowing down whenever one of the familiar sale-boards showed at the roadside, and running on again in response to his laconic, "Give it a pass."

It must have been half-past four when they came to an old-fashioned house, not very large, but of a mellowed dignity, which enabled it to sustain the name of "Cheshurst Hall," without provoking any probable ridicule.

"Brake here." said Mr. Starr, at the first glance, and after reading a board that announced that it was for sale, with fifteen acres of pasture and woodland, they pushed open a pair of infirm gates, and ran the car up a long, weed-grown drive, over which the trees were joining branches, too low for the easy passage of a larger vehicle.

An iron bell clanged vainly through the empty halls, but they were fortunately observed by a gardener who had made some pretence of curbing the disorder of the neglected gardens during the past two years, in return for the right to live rent-free in a cottage on the property, and to take what toll he could of peach-house and vinery.

He fetched a key, showing neglected rooms, with windows cobwebbed, and blinded by outer growths, but dirt and gloom could not hide the beauty of their proportions, and the floors of polished oak, and the dark carved mantels.

"It's been a lovely place," Cora said, thinking that it would be ecstasy to be mistress of such a house, and yet putting it in the past, with practical eyes for the lack of many things that are to be found in a modern cottage, and of the labour which would be needed for the rambling flag-floored kitchens.

"Like it?" said Mr. Starr.

"Yes, of course. But that's not the question. It's you that would have to live here. It would cost a lot to keep up."

"I don't see why it need."

"Well, you will, if you come to live here. Still, I don't want to advise you. It's your matter, not mine."

"I'm not so sure about that."

With this cryptic remark, Mr. Starr turned, and went out into the broader light of the back yard. He must see the land. The gardener led them through the fifteen acres. The gardens were large, and had an ancient beauty which neglect could not quickly obliterate. There was more woodland than pasture, with an intersecting stream, and a shadowed lake at its farther boundary.

The men walked ahead, the gardener pointing out the features of the property Cora lagged somewhat, her mind intrigued by Mr. Starr's last remark.

It was a queer thing for this single man, having no ties in this country, not even admitting that he planned a permanent residence, to wish to buy such a house, and to show such haste.

Was he looking for a mistress for it also, with an equal impetuosity?

It was absurd to suppose that he had developed the idea during the morning. It must have been formed in his mind before he met her. Still, she had been useful to drive him. He might easily have thought of her in a more permanent relationship. The remark *was* hard to interpret otherwise. And yet, being more shrewd than vain, she did not feel satisfied. There must be some other explanation of this headlong search for a country home. Something that she did not know. He was coming back through the bracken, at his briskest pace, leaving the gardener in his rear.

He did not slacken when he came up to her, but only called out, Come along, Miss Pratt; we've got to look alive. There's only just time. It's the second turn to the left after the canal-bridge, and a six-mile run to the town. Sharpe and Headley, in the High Street, just beyond the Cross, on the right. They close at six, so we've got twenty minutes, near enough."

"We can do that," she said, and was silent till they were clear of the drive, and running smoothly on a straight road. Then she asked, "Do you know what that place is worth?"

"No. Do you?"

"Did you learn what they're asking?"

"Yes: £5,000, but the man said they'd take 4,500. It's been empty for two years."

"They'd take three."

"Think so? I'll try. But I'm going to be in tomorrow, if it costs double."

"So it will, if you tell them that."

"Miss Pratt, you must think I'm a mug."

Cora laughed. "Most men are."

"Well, you just sit back and watch."

They said no more till they pulled up opposite a sedate and ancient building, with a small brass plate at the side of a door that opened on to the street of the little country town to which they had been directed.

"Sharpe and Headley," he read. "Here we are. You'd better come in with me, Miss Pratt. You understand these things better than I do."

Cora smiled inwardly at the idea of herself as an expert in the purchase of country houses, but she followed him in.

They were soon seated in the private room of Mr. Gabriel Thompson, the head of the firm, which was of too ancient a respectability to be entitled with the names of its living partners.

Mr. Thompson was a gentleman with a bald head fringed with white, a somewhat weather-reddened face, and an air of urbane precision, the whole effect being that of a lawyer who had deserted his profession for the pursuit of agriculture, or of a farmer who had preferred the law.

"I understand," he said, looking from one to the other in a shrewd-eyed attempt to ascertain their relative importance, and present or prospective relationships, "that you wish to see me about Cheshurst Hall. A very beautiful old property. One of the best in the district that has fallen vacant for many years."

"I wouldn't say *fallen*," Mr. Starr interjected, in the tone of one who will be just, even to the loss of his own pocket. He implied that the property was not suffering from dissolution, but merely from senile decay.

Mr. Thompson looked somewhat disconcerted at this flippancy. He recognized a faint American accent. Probably an eccentric. Doubtless a wealthy one. All Americans are.

He looked at Cora again, in an endeavour to probe the relationship of the visitors. The women are usually so much more important in these negotiations. He wished she would move her hand. The rings (if any) might tell him much, if he could see them.

Cora took his glance as an invitation to speech. She felt that Mr. Starr's point was a good one, but might have been put more tactfully.

She said, "We understand that it has been empty for nearly two years."

"Yes," said her companion. "Two years this fall."

Mr. Thompson looked at him suspiciously. What did he imply now? Then he remembered having read that fall is American for autumn.

"Yes," he said. "Between one and two years. There have been some very good offers for the property. Very good offers. But Lady Blessingford has been rather difficult. Lady Blessingford is very particular in regard to the social amenities of the neighbourhood. Of course, in your case, there would be no difficulty. None at all."

Cora wondered what could be the credentials of their practically anonymous call which could "of course" defeat the scruples of this over-particular female. She decided that it must be her companion's accent. We must be careful not to admit one of a lower social status to purchase residential properties which adjoin our own. But this does not apply to an American. He is of no status whatever, either high or low. He is a permissible freak.

"What's her figure?" said Mr. Starr, who felt that the interview dragged.

Mr. Thompson looked bewildered for a moment. She was a lady of very ample circumference. But he was very far from being a fool.

"The price of the property is £5,000."

Mr. Starr leaned his elbows on the table. He looked into Mr. Thompson's eyes with a hard and holding glance.

"See here, mister," he said, "I've seen the land, and the old shack, and I'm here to buy. I've got to buy a house before I go back tonight, and it's getting on."

Mr. Thompson looked at the clock on the opposite wall. It was six-fifteen. (These eccentric Americans!)

Mr. Starr continued, "I'm here to buy. I'll give you 15,000. That's dollars. I'll give you £3,000 for a quick deal, with no extras. Not a cent more."

Mr. Thompson's face gave no indication of his thoughts. He rang for his clerk, and had a file brought in.

After a moment's reference, he said, "It seems to be a simple title. There's a tithe-charge of £2 13s. per annum. I don't suppose you'd mind that. You could have it commuted, if you wished."

"So could the lady," Mr. Starr replied. "If I buy, I'll buy clear. I'm offering you a good price."

"It's a very low price," the agent answered. "I don't know that she'll consider it at all, but I can submit it, and let you know, if you'll kindly leave me your address"

"I don't buy unless I buy now. If you can't deal, we'll soon hunt her up, if she's located round here."

"She wouldn't do business with you, if you did. She would refer you to us."

"Well, here we are."

"If Lady Blessingford is in residence—perhaps you will wait a few minutes. I may be able to obtain her instructions." (He was thinking, "Would it be any use to stand out for a higher figure?" The bank's charge was about £2,000. Beyond that, the money would be very useful indeed. The finances of Lady Blessingford were complicated by an affection for continental casinos, which was very worrying to those who had the responsibility of her business interests.)

He went into another room, from which they could hear his voice at times, though not in words, in telephonic communication with his titled client.

Then he came back, to resume his seat, saying, as he did so, "I have been bound to advise Lady Blessingford that I regard the price you offer as an extremely low one—as quite inadequate. But I am pleased to be able to tell you that I have her instructions to accept it." (What she had said was, "Now, Thompson, don't be such a fool as to let him go.") "I presume that you would like me to draw a form of contract now, and to take your deposit upon it?"

"I'm here to deal."

Mr. Thompson drew out a sheet of foolscap, and picked up his pen.

"I'll pay you three hundred now, and the whole wad in a week's time. All I want now is the transfer form, showing what it's to cost, and a receipt for what I'm paying now, so that I can take possession in the morning."

"You can't possibly do that," said Mr. Thompson.

Argument followed.

Mr. Starr mentioned that in *his* country there was hardly anything that he couldn't get, if he paid a ten percent deposit.

Mr. Thompson said it was much the same here, but land was different.

Mr. Starr said yes, it *was* different, because it was particularly difficult to get away with it. Anyway, he would have possession tomorrow, or he wouldn't buy.

More telephoning. First to Lady Blessingford, who was found to be in entire agreement with Mr. Starr. If he were buying the place, why keep it standing empty, while the professional gentlemen were running up their bills? And then to her lawyer, Mr. Talkingbooth, who said plainly that he would undertake no responsibility for so monstrous a procedure. Possession on completion, of course. That would be a matter of a month or six weeks, depending partly upon the expedition of Mr. Starr's solicitors. Who were they? He hadn't mentioned any? Then the first thing to do was to get him to name them. Did he think he was buying pork? *They'd* know how to talk some sense into him.

"Well, of course, you're right," said Mr. Thompson uncertainly, "but I don't want to lose him. You know Harris's offer of £1,400 to pull the house down and rebuild is the best we've had since last autumn. I wish we'd closed with Simpson when we had the chance. But it's no use talking about that now. Lady Blessingford won't forgive us, if we let him go. You know he's an American. They will hustle."

Mr. Talkingbooth admitted that. But this was worse than hustling. It was gross indecency. "If you've got to do it, Thompson," he concluded, "the less I know about it the better. And the more informal, the better too. You've got a better chance of wriggling out, if you want to later. Goodness knows what complications'll follow. I never heard of such a thing in my life. I don't suppose there's a lawyer in England who ever did."

Mr. Thompson, receiving banknotes for £300, must draw the required document as best he could, or as Mr. Starr required, and Mr. Starr, knowing little of English law, would leave nothing to be supposed. He would have it very plain indeed, in such explicit words as would have been a fresh affront to Mr. Talkingbooth's legal mind.

Also, he would have it clear that the costs should come out of the £3,000. He didn't care how much Mr. Thompson made out of the deal, but it wouldn't come out of *him*.

Mr. Thompson explained that he should charge Lady Blessingford. Mr. Starr would have to pay Mr. Talkingbooth. But that proved to be a mistake. Mr. Starr would pay his own lawyer, if he had one, but not hers. Mr. Starr had his way.

It was nearly half-past seven when they left the office, and Mr. Starr said, "I must have another look at that place. I want to take the key back in my pocket. There'll be hours of light yet. You don't mind, do you?"

"I don't mind for myself," Cora answered, though she was conscious of an increasingly urgent appetite, "but I've got a brother who will. He'll be home by now, and probably ringing up the police in about ten seconds."

Mr. Starr considered this.

"I see. 'Any more bodies in Bodmin House?' He'd go on that lay, would he? Reckon you're about right. Better ring him up now."

Cora agreed. They drove to the local post office, and got through in a few minutes. She said simply that she was having an evening out, and might be home rather late. Where was she? She mentioned Lady Blessingford, with a vague mendacity. Yes, perfectly, thanks. Coming home by car. How had he got on? Rotten? "So sorry, Ted."

She rang off. Explanations could wait. If the puma had gained possession of an empty house so that he could bury her in the cellar, she was certainly doing all she could to assist the crime.

"It's like," she said, "what they call being an accessory before the event. I expect I'm criminally liable if I get killed. Seven years' penal, as like as not."

Unfortunately, she had said it aloud. Explanations were not easy. Still, they were well received. Mr. Starr seemed to enjoy the joke. If he had any serious intentions of rape and murder, it must have seemed a good one, though rather complicated.

He changed the subject at last by asking if the Major were always out till that hour.

Cora was glad to explain. It gave a reason for his existence, apart from those professional activities which she was not anxious to mention. But she did not expect her auditor to be really interested. Cricket is not a popular American game.

But Mr. Starr had familiarized himself with it already. He had attended more than one match. He surprised her by expressing a warm approval. He had grasped much of its technique, even its phraseology. It was a good game, well played.

Only, its organizers needed more pep. He pointed out that it is no fair test of ability for batsmen to play against different bowlers. There should be a selection of the best bowlers, against whom, say, three of the best bats of each county should play in turn. All the bowling should be done from one end. A mechanical bowling apparatus would be better still. Fielders should be separate experts, and should serve both sides. Like caddies. The competitions should be the same as in football. It was silly to talk about first- and second-class counties that never altered or met. He supposed that those who W ere first-class now daren't risk anything. Just cold feet. Not much sport about *that*.

He might have gone on longer, but they were back at the gate of his new property, and smaller matters left his mind.

CHAPTER XX.

IT was considerably after eleven when Cora, having suffered no violence on their return to the empty residence, and having done the return journey without incident when Mr. Starr had been reluctantly persuaded to leave his purchase, got out at the door of her own flat, and passed the steering-wheel into the hands of its owner, who appeared to have forgotten his profession of incapacity to deal with a right-hand drive.

"I've got to thank you, Miss Pratt, for all the help you've given. I shouldn't have got that place today but for you. I should have gone another way, and got nothing, or something worse. I hope you won't mind running me out again in the morning. There's nothing to do yet at the office, and won't be for another week."

"Well, I don't know," she answered. "We'll talk about that tomorrow. But I've got to thank you for a good—lunch."

That sounded a very nice thing to say, but there was an inflection of the last word that vaguely troubled his mind. He was passing Hyde Park before the idea entered that English women might be in the habit of taking more than two meals a day. At which time Cora was saying, "You needn't look at me like that, Ted, if I am wolfing the ham. I suppose I'd read before now that pumas only feed about three times a week, but it never really came home to me till today. If he thinks I'm going through that again tomorrow, he's just wrong. I should faint at the wheel."

But she was sated at last, and prepared to deal with her brother's inarticulate impatience.

"I didn't promise to tell you anything, Ted; and I didn't suppose that there'd be anything much to tell. Not the first day anyway. But things have moved a bit. And I don't see why I shouldn't tell you the lot.

"So you see," she concluded, "I haven't had a dull day, if it has been a bit short in the victuals. And I don't think there'll be any more gory crime, unless he finds out what your job really is. I wouldn't answer for that. Ted, I could marry that man, if I wanted to."

"Marry *that*—"

"Yes. Marry. Holy matrimony, you know, and all that sort of thing. Met on Thursday morning. Home bought in the afternoon. Married during the weekend. A bit slow, of course; but that's how Britishers are. Everyone knows that."

"Cora," said her brother, roused to seriousness, "it isn't only that he's an American, of whom we know very little, and nothing good. It's that ugly murder you mustn't forget. He was the last man there, and he's the one who's picking up the insurance now. It's through that that he's been buying that house today. It's a marvel that he isn't in jail waiting his trial. I believe it was only Crowther's idea that there were two of them that saved him from arrest, though there's not much logic in that, when you come to think...."

"Well, if he did shoot him, it might have been worse."

"I don't know what you mean."

"Well, he might have tried, and missed, mightn't he? You don't want me to marry a fool."

"I don't want you to marry anyone."

"Well, perhaps I do. And, besides, he could talk to you when you came to see us at weekends. He understands cricket."

"That he doesn't. No American ever did."

"Yes, they do. They play it in Philadelphia. You know that as well as I do. How did you get on, really?"

The Major passed her an evening paper without explanation. She read that Sussex had been batting all day, and that a well-set bat had been twice missed, "once by Cattell-Pratt at mid-on, and, etc."

"What rotten luck," she said. "Was it a sitter?"

No. It appeared that it was no better than a libel. It had not been a chance at all.

"I don't know how it looked from the press-box, but the ball didn't come within two yards of any possibility of getting to it. No one could have caught it that ever lived," said the wretched man.

Cora knew her brother well enough to recognize this for truth. He would be very unlikely to excuse himself for a real failure.

Yet why worry? Everyone misses a catch at times. But the point was that he had the reputation of a poor fielder. Nothing was more likely to keep him out of the team than a criticism of that kind. He was not careless. He did his best. That was the most hopeless feature of the case.

It needed no explanation for Cora to understand. There could be no consolation to offer. She went on hurriedly to describe Mr.

Starr's suggestion that, if some men were played separately as fielders only, it would improve the gladiatorial possibilities of the game.

The Major rose readily to the bait. The laws of cricket are too sacred to be lightly altered. But reverent minds may toy for a moment with an impious thought.

He instanced the case of Mundy Wypers—Edmund had been his original name—who was played by his own club for his slip-fielding. He was a man as near seven feet as six, with huge hands, who could leap several feet into the air, or sideways, for the fast ball that glances from the bat's edge. He was equal to any two in the slips. In combination with a fast bowler, sending down going-away balls, he was the terror of opposing sides; but when he went to the wicket, he couldn't hit a long-hop. It was said of him that he had only played a ball once in his life, and then he had turned it into his own stumps.

But if fielders should become a separate caste, he would be an international in a week.

"There's another thing I might tell you," Cora remarked, when the prolific subject of fielding showed signs of death, "Mr. Trentham's very fair in a deal. I don't believe he'd cheat anyone; not to matter, that is. I don't mean stockbrokers, and banks, and people like that."

Her brother looked his exasperation. "If this is the result," he said, "of one day of a criminal atmosphere—! Do you want to be another Chicago May?"

"Oh, I don't know," she said carelessly. "It might be rather fun"; and before he could think of any adequate answer, she had retired for the night.

Left alone thus, he knocked out his pipe thoughtfully. No doubt, she had had an exciting day. He must talk to her in the morning, when she would be more like her normal self. For this thing had got to stop.

CHAPTER XXI.

CORA, though somewhat more vivacious and volatile than her brother, was fundamentally of a direct and practical mind.

She lay awake in the early hours of the summer morning considering the incidents of the previous day, and endeavouring to analyse her own feelings towards the acquaintance that she had formed.

She was not greatly concerned to know whether, or to what degree, he might have been associated with Mr. Bulfwin's very violent end. Men have killed men in considerable numbers, and in great variety of circumstance, during the centuries of recorded history, but it has never been observed that they experienced any consequent difficulty in obtaining wives. The evidence is, indeed, somewhat heavily in the other scale.

But Miss Cattell-Pratt was aware that she had encountered a man of an unusual type, or, at least, that was unusual to her; and she was not yet of an infatuation to blind her to the consideration of how far they were likely to be of a permanent compatibility.

She recognized a quality in him which was formidable, if not dangerous, though she was not aware that she feared it. She felt it rather to be at her service and appreciated it as of the nature of a protection rather than a threat.

She was conscious also of his youth. There was a very boyish quality in Mr. Starr's impetuosities. In the buying of the house....

Her mind wandered to the realization that she would like to be the mistress of Cheshurst Hall. How much was she in love with it, and how much—or how little—could she be with its headlong owner?

She wondered again at the energy of the imprudent purchase. She would have liked to think that it was their meeting that had inspired him with the sudden resolution to find a home that he could offer her, but, as before, she was not disposed to admit the adequacy of that explanation.

There was something that she did not know, some hidden purpose.

Another woman? The probability of that explanation was an unwelcome shock. Anyway, the genuine, boyish delight in his acquisition was a fact beyond question. She was sure that he would want to return there today, and she had little doubt that she would be asked to go with him. The probability was not unpleasing, but in future she would take a lunch-basket in the car. No more puma habits for her!

And there would be Ted to be dealt with first.

Energy waked with the thought. She drew up a leg, and with one vigorous kick threw the bed-clothes over the bottom-rail, swung her feet on to the floor, and walked to the window. The lobelias and white and scarlet geraniums in the window-box, which had been pale with dust yesterday morning, were now green and heavy with clinging rain. Ted would be wild! Still it might clear. Rain before seven—she knew the proverb. But was it really before seven? Daylight-saving is so confusing. What had the ghost said when it struck twelve? "Only eleven o'clock swanking." Did that mean that it was earlier or later by sun time now? Anyway, there wasn't any. It would probably clear before eleven, and Middlesex could bat on a dead wicket, and put their opponents in when the sun came out. That would be the right thing to tell Ted. She heard a movement in the next room, and a slow yawn shut down abruptly, as she made a dash for the bathroom. He could wait five minutes much better than she could wait for half an hour.

"It's no use looking like that," she said, as the Major left his bacon, for the second time in three minutes, to gaze at the strip of leaden sky which was visible from the window. "There's lots of time for it to clear, and if it does, you'll probably go in and make a duck, and wish it hadn't. And then," she added, audaciously bringing up the subject which she knew must be faced before she left the flat, "you oughtn't to care about a little thing like that, when your only sister's going forth to be buried alive, or garrotted, or something equally horrible."

"Then you shouldn't go," he answered, with an unusual irritation. "You know it's a crack-brained thing to do. And what shall we be like here in a month, if you go off every day like that?"

"I know I've got to get some more help, if it lasts," she answered, in a more serious voice, "but it hardly seems real, as yet; and I didn't want to do anything in a hurry. If it does last, we can afford it out of what I shall get. And really, Ted, you can't think that

Mr. Trentham has a habit of murdering his secretaries before they begin to work."

"It isn't only him, it's that Yankee crook."

"I gathered that," she answered, with her dimple showing, "and I suppose it's no use pointing out that he's no more a Yankee than you're a Highlander; that we've not the faintest reason to think he's a crook; and that, if he were, or if he did kill that man Bulfwin, who was, it's no reason why he should commit homicide on the office-staff, that's done nothing worse than drive his two-seater."

"You can rot as much as you like," he answered stubbornly, "but it doesn't alter it that they're not the sort for you to mix up with. If you want to take on office work, why not go somewhere respectable?"

"Because I'd rather go somewhere interesting, I suppose. But really, Ted, I'll throw it up if it turns out like you think. But it seems straight enough now, and it's good pay, and—"

But the Major had given up the argument and left the room.

CHAPTER XXII.

THE instructions that Cora had received from the directors of Bulfwin's Syndicate did not include any precise requirements as to the office hours that she should observe. She felt at liberty, therefore, after the toils and privations of the previous evening, to dispose of her domestic responsibilities without any unseemly haste, before setting out for Bodmin House.

It was consequently mid-morning when she arrived at that important building, and she was not, perhaps, excessively surprised to observe a two-seater car standing against the curb, without human attendance, but in a condition which could not properly be described as unoccupied.

Her resolution to apply her considerable natural ability, and somewhat meagre secretarial training, to the subjection of the Share Register died a natural death as she entered the office, and Mr. Starr rose eagerly to his feet with the exclamation, "Miss Pratt, I thought you'd never come. Trentham's just phoned that he won't be in to-day. There's nothing to keep you here worth a dime. I've got the car down below."

"Yes, I saw that. I don't think you're allowed to park cars in this street. You'll get a summons if you leave it like that. This isn't the Wild West."

"No, nor N'York either, or they'd have pulled me in before now. I shan't have one summons. I shall have four or five. I forget which.

"There's one thing. I've given a different name every time an officer came up. Trentham first, and then Mortimer, and then Kingsley, and Lytton. I haven't given Starr yet, so it can't be more than four. That's not so bad. I shall have to do a quick change in the wings between each, when they come on."

Cora laughed at an irresponsibility beside which the buoyancy of her own youth felt itself to be of an almost matronly sedateness. After all, he was no more than a boy in years—a boy whose natural alertness and gaiety of mind had been tempered in a hard and probably lawless school. She was not in a mood for any severity of criticism.

It may have been the sense of his youth, or the effect of the subconscious comradeship which brought his hand to her arm as he drew her from the door toward the waiting lift, that caused her to use his Christian name as she answered:

"I'm afraid, Kingsley, you haven't done yourself much good by giving different names. They'll see the car's the same number every time."

He disregarded the probable result of his assertion of quadruple personalities, with an instant recognition of her more familiar mode of address.

"You're not going to be as standoffish as yesterday? That's great. I just hated calling you Miss Pratt."

Cora said nothing to this, and they reached the street together to find a watery sunlight patterning the still wet pavements, but her quick thought of pleasure on her brother's behalf was abruptly terminated by the sight of a rather portly constable standing beside the car, in the act of pulling the elastic strap from his notebook.

"Traffic cop number five." Mr. Starr was confidentially cheerful. And then to the constable, "Guess it's the old tale. I'm the owner of this bus. Starr's the name. Lytton K. Starr."

The policeman looked puzzled. He glanced at a note of an hour ago. The car was certainly the same. He had already checked that. The owner appeared to be the same, as was natural enough. But the name wasn't.

"I thought you were Mr. Kingsley, sir," he began in respectful but definite accusation.

What reply he would have received will never be known, for Cora interposed quickly:

"Mr. Starr—Mr. Lytton Kingsley Starr's an American. We call him Mr. Kingsley more often than not, but it's all the same. He couldn't understand he was doing anything wrong, till I explained it just now. He's a native of Chickadee. They leave their cars just where they like there. In the very middle of the main street, more often than not. Don't they, Mr. Kingsley?"

"It isn't only the car, miss," said the constable, in what she felt to be a much more satisfactory tone, "it's all this being left." He indicated, with a large hand, a pile of parcels and packages which suggested a coming difficulty in the loading-up of its human freight. "It isn't a right thing to do, miss. Not in a street like this."

"No. It isn't like Chickadee," Cora agreed seriously. "I don't suppose they'd touch anything there, if it were left for a week. They're too busy shooting each other up. But it's very good of you to have watched them for us. I think, Kingsley, you ought to give the officer something for that." A note passed with a celerity suggesting that Mr, Starr was not as completely out of touch with such episodes in his native land as Cora's imagination had indicated.

"Look here, Cop," he said, with a burst of candour, "that car's been in trouble all morning. You might tell the others how it is. I've just been waiting for this lady to come, and when you're expecting to get married in the afternoon, you can't think of a little thing like that."

"No, sir," said the now-beaming constable, with a look of admiration at a silent and confounded Cora, "I don't see as how you could, sir. Thank you, sir. I'll see what I can do."

He closed the door upon the two, who were now tightly wedged among the pile of parcels, and the car moved off.

CHAPTER XXIII.

IT may have been nothing more than the natural duplicity of her sex, to which we have already made discreet allusion, that enabled Cora to preserve an outward coolness of demeanour, the while her heart was beating so that she felt that it must be audible above the noise of the car and the surrounding traffic, but it was an individual audacity that caused her to turn to her companion (not without difficulty, so tightly were they wedged together) and say: "You'd better tell me just what the programme is. If you want me to run out to Cheshurst Hall before the interesting event you mentioned, we haven't much time to lose."

Mr. Starr looked puzzled. She found it necessary to be more explicit.

"I thought you said you were going to be married this afternoon. You mayn't know, but there's a time limit in this country. It used to be three o'clock once, but it may have changed. It's not a subject I know much about."

"What a silly idea! Still, we've got time. It's only eight minutes to eleven now."

"It's also usual to make a definite appointment for those occasions. When is she expecting you to turn up?"

"It isn't she. It's us."

"When are we expecting her to turn up then?"

"You know I didn't mean that."

Cora was cooler now. She was inwardly enjoying herself quite as much as she deserved, and perhaps more. She only wished that the event had been more spaciously staged. She saw that her dignity might require her to quarrel at any moment, and it's not an easy thing to do while you're steering a Morris-Cowley two-seater through the congestion of the London traffic, and wedged so closely to your opponent that you have difficulty in getting sufficient freedom for your left elbow.

She said, "I don't want to ask you anything you'd rather not tell me. Only, if you want to be driven to Cheshurst Hall before the ceremony, it's just as well to know how much time I've got. And you'll have to let me know where it's to be, sooner or later, unless you're going to drive there by yourself, and I'm to walk home."

"I don't care whether we go to Cheshurst Hall before or not, but you know there won't be any ceremony if you're not there."

"Really?" he said, with a well-simulated note of wonder in her voice. "I didn't know that I was as important as that. I've never been a bridesmaid yet, and I'm not sure that I want to try."

"We don't want any bridesmaids. Two's enough for getting married where I come from."

"If you're meaning me, Mr. Starr, I'm afraid you'll be one fewer than that."

"Well, I call that real mean. When I've got you that house and all. I reckoned we'd get the furniture loaded up this afternoon, and sort it out over tomorrow, and be all straight for Sunday. You know that's what it's got to come to, so what's the use of wasting the day?"

"I don't know anything of the kind." She twisted round, so that she could face him squarely. "No. Don't do that. Keep your arm to itself, or you'll have a smash." The car swerved to the curb, and then abruptly took the crown of the road. Her eyes met his with an angry courage, and with a resolution no less than his own. "You may marry every girl you meet in Chickadee within twenty-four hours, for all I know, and give her up a day later, but we've different ways here. We only get married quite occasionally," she concluded, with a return to her lighter manner, "and it often lasts quite a time."

"Cora," he answered, with a boyish plaintiveness in his voice, which showed how far he was tamed already, "don't be a beast. You know I never married anyone. I've never even kissed a girl in my life. I never wanted to till I met you."

It was a statement which has been made to a good many women under more or less similar circumstances, though it may be less often believed than its authors suppose, but Cora, though she cannot be classed among the most credulous of her sex, was more than half-inclined to do so.

She did not consider that he was incapable of fluent and resolute lying, but she thought she knew when he spoke with sincerity. Inwardly relentful, she froze again when he added, with an amazing impudence, "At least, not to matter."

He saw the effect of his words with an evident consternation, but made no effort either to explain or withdraw them; only adding, in a tone which had become sulky, in reaction to her own aloofness, "To turn on me like this, when I've just got you the house and all, and we might have had a good time!"

It is possible that she might have replied in a more complaisant temper, had she not recalled her conviction that he had bought the house with some quite different purpose.

"Look here, Kingsley," she said resolutely. "You're not a bad sort and I don't want to quarrel on a day like this, but you'd have a better chance with me if you'd tell the truth, and not think I'm a fool. You didn't get that house for me, and it would be just as well to be frank and say why you did."

There was no answer to this. He was not only silenced, but disconcerted to a degree that appeared reasonless.

She had slowed down, having some respect for her own safety, as the quarrel rose, but now she changed gear and addressed herself to the speedy transit of the bypass road. They ran on for two or three miles before he spoke, and then it was only to ask, "You don't want to marry a fool, do you?"

"Not so urgently that it can't wait."

"Well, you would, if I did."

"Marry a fool, if you married me?"

"You know I didn't mean that. I mean that I should be the fool if you didn't."

"You may think you mean something, but I've no idea what it is."

"It's plain enough. There are lots of things I can tell you tomorrow, if we're married today. But I'd be a fool if I blabbed it all out and you walked off."

"I've not asked you to tell me anything. I've only asked you not to tell me things that aren't true. I said you didn't buy the house for me, and I suppose this is how you own up."

Silence again. It appeared to be a subject that could always be used to terminate conversation, should she desire a pause.

After a time she reopened it herself with the remark: "If you'd known more of the marriage laws of this country, you wouldn't have proposed something that you couldn't have done, even if it hadn't been so absurd. You can't marry any moment you like here."

"Is it as bad as a house?" he inquired, with interest. "I got over that, anyway."

Cora considered the point before answering. Her knowledge of either marriage or property laws was not extensive, but she was inclined to the opinion that the legal barriers to the speedy acquisition of a wife may be more expeditiously surmounted under most circumstances than those that guard the more substantial asset. Still, having seen the one give way before her companion's impetuosity, it would never do to say that a wife could be obtained more easily or expeditiously than *that*.

She evaded the issue with some adroitness.

"I don't say which is the worse, but you didn't buy a house yesterday. You only paid a deposit. You can't get a wife on the hire-purchase. I believe it takes three weeks with banns, and less with a licence, but I don't know how much. There's a more important difference than that. The law doesn't fix the date."

"It's a rotten hold-up. And that cop at the lock-up said it was a civilized country! I'll get the licence this afternoon. I suppose you know where to go?"

"It's just as well to get the wife first."

"I suppose you think that I shouldn't feed you."

"I hadn't thought about that. It is a bit of a risk, isn't it?"

"I'm real sorry. But you might have said something. I was only thinking about the house. I'll give you half the cash at the start. You won't need to starve on that. Nor today, either. There's about $30.00 of good feed on this bus."

"Do you mean that these parcels are all food? Did you expect me to eat them all on the way out?"

"Not the lot. But there'd be more room if you would."

"Would there? I don't see...Well, anyway I'm not going to start."

"I suppose you'll guy me about yesterday till we're both dead."

"One less than that," she answered lightly, and fell into a thoughtful silence. She did not fail to observe that she had been offered a somewhat substantial marriage settlement, accompanied by a rather attractive and quite harmless husband. Yes, quite. Rather young, but there are worse faults. She hated dullness, and she didn't think that he was likely to offer her a dull life. Ted's face, "if she should go home, and say that the deed was done!" But she wasn't going to be married, either this week or next. She meant to have some fun first, and some time to make up her mind.

The car turned into the narrower lanes, and she must concentrate upon the more immediate responsibility.

CHAPTER XXIV.

THEY were within a mile of their destination, at the foot of one of those steep and shaded hills which are characteristic of the wooded lanes of Kent, when the car stopped. A brief examination revealed that it was suffering from an empty tank.

Cora, still seated among the parcels, looked speculatively at her companion. He hadn't seemed as surprised as might reasonably have been expected.

She did not think seriously that he had planned to delay her in this lonely place. She knew that cars with a single female occupant usually break down about 10:00 P.M. in the summer months. Besides, she was convinced of his anxiety to reach his new residence.

Yet there were circumstances which invited further inquiry. "You seemed to know where to look," she said pleasantly.

"Meaning?"

"You didn't seem as surprised as you might have done, considering that we had that tank filled to the brim about five minutes before we got to Knightsbridge last night. What sort of a place did you put it up in?"

"I wasn't."

"Wasn't what?"

"Wasn't surprised. But I ought to have remembered."

Cora made no answer. She looked at him as one who waits. After a moment's silence he went on:

"I've been out in the night. Out to the Hall, I mean. I took some things."

"I suppose that accounts for it."

"Yes, of course."

"Accounts for what?"

"The petrol, of course."

"I don't mean that."

"I don't know what you do mean."

"The way you've been going on about marriage licences. I expect you need sleep. You'll feel better tomorrow."

"I wish you wouldn't rag all the time. I shan't feel better tomorrow, if I haven't got it. I shall feel a lot worse. The question is how we're to get any juice for this bus."

"I wasn't ragging." She had abstracted herself from the parcels by this time, and stood beside him in the road. It didn't seem much use to go on sitting there. "I meant every word I said. You can't push it up this hill. We've got to go and get some petrol; it won't come to us; and I'm the chauffeuse, so I suppose 'us' means 'me,' I suppose," she added innocently, "a right-hand drive comes easier in the dark."

He looked puzzled for a moment, and then his eyes hardened to a sudden unexpected anger.

"Look here, Miss Pratt, if you're coming spying on me—" he commenced, and then checked abruptly, but his face did not clear. He looked at her in a way that was half-sulky and half-suspicious, and altogether resentful.

She wondered what could be the secret of his nocturnal wandering which could rouse him to that distrustful anger, but it was his business, not hers. Perhaps, she thought, she ought to thank it for a timely warning. Fortified by these reflections, she answered easily: "If you are a puma, I don't see why you should be a pig. I don't care if you really can drive right-hand in the dark, and can't in the day, but if you like to be your own chauffeur, I wish you'd remember when to fill the tank. Anyway, if you want to look silly quarrelling in the road, you might as well wait till he's close enough to hear what you say."

His anger collapsed as quickly as it had risen, before her refusal to respond to his own temperature. It had been one of those moments that may settle the reaction of two people to each other for many future years.

"I wish I sometime's new what you meant," he said, in a tone that was apologetic for all its sulkiness. He looked up the hill, and observed a rather tall and ample man descending towards them. His dress indicated one of the pillars of the Anglican Church, and his dignity suggested that he had long forgotten how a curate feels. He was the rector of the parish of Little Hempstill, of which Cheshurst Hall is a conspicuous and ancient ornament.

He paused on reaching them, with an air of condescending benevolence, and inquired the cause of the trouble. Having learnt it, he was sympathetic, but not encouraging. It was a choice of waiting there—and it might be hours before another car came along—or of walking back nearly two miles. There was no hope in going forward. There was nothing that way but some cottages and an empty house—Cheshurst Hall—at least, he had just heard that it had been bought by an eccentric American millionaire. But there was no one but a gardener there now. At last, under the influence of the ardent interest of his auditors, and being very well used to the sound of his own voice, he became garrulous.

At least, there ought to be no one there. The American had not moved in. He understood that the purchase had not been completed till yesterday, But he had just met Menzies (that was the gardener), who had told him that he was not only certain that he had seen a ghost there (if not two) during the night, which might happen to anyone, but he was sure that someone was concealed in the house at the present moment. He could not open the doors, as he had handed the keys to the new owner yesterday, but he had been intending to fetch a ladder to investigate the mystery through an upper window.

"The damned meddling swine!"

It was Mr. Starr's expletive, and the rector looked startled, as was natural; and shocked, as was professionally necessary.

"I don't see what—" he began, and Cora interrupted him with her usual readiness.

"You mustn't talk like that, Kingsley. It isn't done before clergymen. Besides, I don't know what swine is in American, but it's plural in English. You see, rector, it's Mr. Starr here who bought the house, and he likes to get through his own windows himself. It really isn't part of a gardener's—"

"The question is," Mr. Starr said impatiently, "just how quick can we get that juice?"

The rector had a new suggestion to offer. There may be limits to the requirements of Christian benevolence as it should be exercised to a young man who swears in the road, but a wealthy and eccentric parishioner must be entered in a very different category.

There was a short cut to the rectory over the fields—not easy to find, but to be traversed in a few minutes if he should show it. He might himself have a gallon which he could spare, if Mr. Starr would walk with him.

Mr. Starr certainly would. He had, indeed, a tendency to walk in front, only partially checked by the difficulty that he didn't know where to go. With that qualification, they went off together.

A very thoughtful Cora got back into the car.

She sat for a few minutes reflecting upon the incidents of the past hour.

She had had an interesting offer of marriage, and she was (or so she thought) upon the threshold of an exciting mystery.

She had a conviction that Kingsley could drive that car quite well, either by night or day, but she was less than sure that he had done so last night. She did not merely suspect mystery; he had admitted it by implication when he had said that he would tell her tomorrow, if they were married today. She supposed that, had she been an American, she would have married him to gratify her curiosity, and divorced him later in the day. If she had told him why she had wedded him, he might have developed sufficient incompatibility of temperament to justify the division. But it was difficult to arrange matters like that in the more stolid land of her birth.

Then there was this tale of someone being in the house. True or false, it had disturbed Kingsley's mind more than was reasonable, if it were empty. He had his feelings well under control in emergencies as a rule, but she had seen that he could not conceal his impatience easily, as he had started away with the rector.

Suppose that there were something in the house that it might be vital to Kingsley's interests, even to his life, to conceal, and which the gardener might, even now, be discovering?

She saw that she might have to choose sides very definitely, and very soon. Should she prefer his, she might be involved at any moment in dangers or illegalities that she could not very easily estimate. Well, if she took his side, he would have to be franker than he was now; and without talk of marrying either. Lots of people had to trust each other who didn't marry. A burglar didn't marry all his pals, or his pals' wives. It was an ominous sign, which she might have noticed more, that her mind, thinking of Kingsley, gravitated naturally to criminal comparisons.

There was no reason that he shouldn't trust her, and yet— She thought of her brother's occupation: of the half-formed purpose with which she had taken the secretarial position which had brought her here. If he should give her his confidence, and then learn.... She did not lack courage, but she felt cold in the sunlight.

Still, if he were frank with her, she could be frank with him. Could she? She did not know what he might have to tell. It might prove an impossible treachery to her brother to reply by revealing his occupation, and the investigation on which he was occupied. On the other hand, it was against Mortimer Trentham that Ted had been instructed to direct his activities. Well, it was no use worrying. She felt some confidence in her capacity to meet the event that came. Neither was she much perturbed by the thought of the gardener's ladder. She had some' confidence in Kingsley's capacity also.

"Even if I don't get married, it's going to be a quite interesting day," she concluded, and this anticipation was not reduced by the sound of a motor-bicycle that came quickly round the bend of the road behind her, and stopped at the side of her car, while the voice of Inspector Cleveland said:

"Good afternoon, Miss Cattell-Pratt. I wonder what you're doing in this part of Kent?"

CHAPTER XXV.

CORA saw that the time for decision had come even more quickly than she had anticipated.

She might say, "Don't stop to talk. If you go on quickly to Cheshurst Hall, you'll have five minutes' start, and the gardener may help you to something interesting."

Or she might simply tell him what had happened, and leave him to his own conclusions and actions, which would probably be just the same, except that the five minutes would have become three.

She took her choice when she answered, "I'm earning four guineas a week, if you want to know. I wonder whether your reason's equally good."

Inspector Cleveland did not enlighten her.

"That's Starr's car," he said definitely. "Where's he gone?"

"He's making a call at the rectory."

The Inspector had made it a matter of facial discipline for many years not to show surprise at anything which he might hear.

He only asked, "Where's that?"

"Sorry, but I don't know. I expect anyone'd tell you round here."

"Which way did he go?"

"Neither. He went over the fields."

Inspector Cleveland made a mistake of which he was seldom guilty. He defeated himself by the subtlety of his own mind. He didn't believe that Starr had gone to the rectory. It wasn't likely. It wasn't sense. And over the fields, too! He diagnosed some secret assignation. Doubtless, Cora was passing on a lie that had been told to her.

He asked, "What's he gone there for?"

"I believe he had an invitation from the rector."

"What's the rector's name?"

"I've no idea."

"Didn't he mention it?"

"Who? Mr. Starr? No, I'm sure he didn't."

"How soon do you expect him back?"

"Any minute, for all I know. I suppose you can guess what he'll think if he finds you here."

"You mean I'm queering the pitch?"

"Not exactly that." She had a scruple of conscience about implying that they were engaged in the same hunt. "I mean, it's risk enough that he'll find out Ted's occupation without you butting in. I don't want to lose this job before I've got the first week's salary."

Inspector Cleveland had no mind to be turned back from the investigation he had in hand. He had learnt enough during the last twenty-four hours to give him a very good appetite for learning more. But he liked Cora, and he did not forget that she was Ted's sister. He saw that it might be risky for her, and no advantage to him, for them to be found together. He did not doubt that she was here to help her brother, and was rather surprised that he should have allowed her to do it.

"Well," he said, "I'd better clear. You won't tell him you've seen me round here?"

Cora had no intention of doing so, but a natural wariness in the use of words, arising from the position in which she was placed, caused her to avoid the direct promise, for which she had reason to be glad afterwards.

"Is it likely?" she said lightly. "But I'm not asking you to linger just now."

"No," he repeated. "I'd better clear. I expect Ted will let me know anything you find out. You'll be back tonight?"

Cora's right hand was on the side of the car as they talked. She lifted it slightly, small and slender, and rather soiled.

"You see that, Inspector?" she asked, with a friendly smile.

The Inspector was a solid rather than a quick-witted man. He did not fail to take her meaning, though he had a moment's thought before he did so.

"You mean you're playing for your own hand?"

"Yes," she said. "Just that. Ted's wild. He thinks I'm in with a gang who murder each other more mornings than not, and going to marry most of them, if I haven't done so already."

The Inspector wheeled his bicycle round. He went back the way he came, though he may not have gone far. Fiction had familiarized him with the amateur detective who will not communicate the results of his skill till he can demonstrate his superior ability to the confounded professional, but he had not thought that Cora would be so silly.

That young lady leaned back in the car, well content that she had delayed his investigations, and that she had defeated him by the confusing quality of selected truths, rather than by any lower form of falsehood.

Her complacency was broken by the voice of Kingsley, who stepped out of the hedge-side with the remark, "I think I've seen that man before."

CHAPTER XXVI.

CORA made no answer, and Kingsley said nothing further, as he hurriedly filled the tank and tumbled into the car.

"Let her out," he said, as the car took the hill well enough on its second gear, and came to an equally abrupt descent.

He sat silent, rather sullen. and obviously impatient and disturbed in mind, leaving Cora to wonder whether it were the possible exploits of the gardener or the sight of her recent companion which was responsible for his moody silence.

Anyway, he had no reason to complain of the pace at which she drove, and she had little time or leisure for speculation before she had turned quickly into the open gates and pulled up before the front of Cheshurst Hall.

It looked quiet and deserted enough, and the operations of the gardener (if any) were not visible from this side of the house.

Kingsley jumped out quickly, pulling a bunch of heavy keys from his hip-pocket.

The green-painted doors, cracked, sun-blistered, and faded, gave a reluctant response to his impetuosity, one of them scraping heavily on the stones of the porch as he forced it open.

He turned in an impatient uncertainty to look back at Cora, who kept her place in the car.

"You'd better—no, you'd better wait there. I shan't be long."

He went in, closing the doors behind him. She heard a bolt grate in the staple.

She was left to reflect on this treatment of one who had been invited an hour ago to come as a bride taking possession of her own home. She supposed accurately enough that she had roused his suspicion by being overseen in conversation with Inspector Cleveland. That, and the report of the gardener's activities, must explain her present exclusion, but how much she should attribute to each event she would have been interested to know. And what mystery could it be that the house held? A house that he had only entered last evening.

Why had he brought her here at all, if he had that within which he must conceal?

Well, she thought she could answer that. He wanted her as a friend. He might be in urgent need of an ally. She had refused his absurd offer of marriage. He had found her in conversation with Inspector Cleveland. He did not know how the disposition of his secret (whatever it might be) might have been disturbed or disclosed by the gardener's meddling. So he preferred to shut her out while he made his investigations.

That was reasonable enough. Anyway, she wouldn't have to wait for ever. He would want to come out for the parcels. And for the same reason, she wouldn't starve. There was the $30.00 worth of food.

She looked up at the ivy-grown uncurtained windows, but she was less fortunate than the gardener. She saw no sign of life at all. Well, there was no hurry. She could wait.

When she had done so for about half an hour, she heard the noise of the creaking bolt, the doors opened, and Kingsley came out.

He unlatched the door of the car for her, saying in a quieter voice than she had been accustomed to hear from him, "I'm sorry you've been kept waiting so long. We'd better get the parcels into the kitchen."

She thought he looked different. Had he changed his clothes? No, or not all. She recognized a mark of dirt on the right sleeve of his jacket. It must be that he had washed. Yes, he looked cleaner than he had before.

But there was one change that was evident. He had become unfriendly and suspicious. As they made the four journeys through the long, cold, stone-paved passages to the kitchen, which were necessary to transfer the contents of the car, she noticed him looking at her more than once with a speculative, even hostile expression. A thought came, half-flippantly, but with a nervous undertone, to which she gave instant voice, with her usual audacity:

"You look as though you'd murder me, if you could only think of the safest way. Do you kill all the girls you don't marry, or marry all the girls you don't kill? Or do you do both to each on the same day?"

She thought he looked startled and disconcerted, in the half-light of the passage in which they spoke, but he did not react as she had expected, either with sudden anger or with his more aggressive moods.

He just looked at her once, and then walked on without answering, and the silence seemed more sinister than an angry word.

When they reached the kitchen, and laid down the last load on a dresser which was built into the wail, she faced him squarely.

"Look here, Mr. Starr, I didn't ask to come here, and I don't want to stay. You can drive just as well as I can, and if you've got something here to hide, I don't know why you asked me to come."

"Neither do I," was the unexpected reply, which he seemed to regret the moment it had passed his lips.

She went on: "Then the only question is how soon I can get away. Are you coming back in the car, or do you expect me to walk? I won't stay here, even if I have to do that. I may be the secretary of Bulfwin's Syndicate, but it's no part of my job to carry your parcels here."

Once again he did not react quite as she expected; he seemed strange and different in a way which she could not define to her own satisfaction, but his tone was more conciliatory as he replied: "I didn't mean to say that. Of course, I wanted you to come. You'll want something to cat before we go back. Let's have a look round first—I want to see that it's all right upstairs—and then we'll have a meal, and get off."

It was awkwardly said, and she had a warning instinct of danger, which she put resolutely behind her. She couldn't really walk home; nor could she take his car, and leave him to do so.

When he repeated, "Come and have a look over the house," she responded with an inward, "Now, Cora, don't be a fool," and an outward readiness, and when he led the way up a wide staircase, with broad and shallow steps of polished oak and carved banisters, she was roused to an admiration which overcame the disquiet that had invaded her mind.

"There's a fine view from here;" he said, opening the door to a spacious bedroom, with a roof that seemed disproportionately low. "You can see miles from the window at the farther end."

He stepped aside for her to enter, and drew the key from the lock as he followed. As she was half across the floor, he turned swiftly and silently backward.

He was on the landing again before she had become aware of his movement, and he would have accomplished his purpose easily enough but that the key did not fit into the lock from the outside.

She looked round to speak as she reached the window, and guessed his purpose instantly when she found that he was no longer beside her. In another second she had recrossed the room, and, as at last he forced the key into its place, and was in the act of turning it, she pulled the door open vigorously.

Anger was stronger than fear in the mood with which she faced him.

"Look here, Kingsley, I'll have none of those games; I'll go home just when...."

Their eyes met, and the sentence died before something which she had not expected, and was not equal to meet.

She knew his sulkiness, and she knew his anger, but in the eyes that met hers there was an hostility, a dislike, which was now unmistakable, and for which she was not prepared.

If this were the real Kingsley, she was in an evil case indeed.

"—when I say you may," he finished for her, "and till then, you'll stay here."

She stepped back before the sudden menace of a pistol barrel, which she did not wish to look down.

"I thought you told me you never carried one of those things here," she said, with a brave attempt at the light tone which she felt to be her strongest weapon for that emergency.

"You think too much," he answered curtly, and drew the door shut again, turning the key before she had gathered courage for further resistance.

CHAPTER XXVII.

Cora returned to the window a deep, curved recess, giving wide views to south and east over a wooded Kentish valley, but she did not go there to admire the' scenery. Its first attraction was in the window-seat that it held, without which she would have been reduced, after a time, to the ignominy of the dusty floor.

She admitted that she was scared, though she told herself that she was foolish to be so. She had thought that she knew Kingsley well enough to have no cause to fear him. Even now, she felt some confidence in her ability to control him, some assurance of his feeling toward herself, till she remembered the look which he had given her at the door. It was not merely that it was hostile or threatening, but that it had been like the gaze of a stranger, such as might be given by one who had become insane, and to whom the dearest of yesterday might have become forgotten or hated.

She supposed that there must be others in the house, and that they had persuaded him to distrust her—might have learnt and told him of her brother's occupation, which would in itself, when considered with her meeting with Inspector Cleveland, be enough to condemn her.

Under such suspicion, she might well be anxious as to the end of her adventure. She could not tell the extent of her peril, for she could not tell the greatness of their own danger. Cruelty is the child of fear, and if their necks were at stake, to what extremity might it not persuade them? If Kingsley himself had condemned her, what verdict, or what fate, could she expect at the hands of the strangers into whose power she supposed that she had fallen?

Tiring of these reflections, she considered the possibilities of escape, to which her thoughts might have turned more promptly had she been either of a more aggressive or a more nervous temperament.

The house was quiet enough to suggest that it had been deserted by those who had confined her to make their escape in safety, but she did not feel confident of this explanation. Could she force the door, which did not appear easy, she must expect to be confronted by an angry Kingsley, and perhaps by others. She had sense enough to avoid appeal to the verdict of violence, unless she could reasonably suppose that it would be favourable to herself. She turned away from the door. Later, perhaps—

The chimney did not attract her. It was of sufficient width, but it would be a very dirty way. It might be easier to get on to the roof than to get off. She could not hope to gain that doubtful measure of freedom without soiled hands and ruined clothes: probably a soot-smeared face, and some absurdity of public rescue. Even for freedom, she would not willingly risk being ridiculous. Later, perhaps—

The windows beside which she had been sitting showed an easier way. There was a casement at each corner of the alcoves, latched on the inside, but not otherwise fastened. It was a first-floor room. Should she lower herself by her hands, it would not be a long drop. There was a Virginia creeper upon the wall, which might aid a still easier descent, though it did not appear capable of sustaining any very considerable weight.

She was tempted here, but even this was a rough and dirty way. She would rely upon arms and legs to make the descent should it be necessary; but she preferred her wits, till they had been more severely tested. Later, perhaps—

There was a sash-window opposite to the door, but the wall beneath it was bare, the ground was lower on that side, and the drop would have been on to the hardness of the gravel drive. She looked at it only to turn away, but she observed that the car still stood before the door. Evidently, they had not locked her there so that they might escape, or they were in no hurry to do so. She reflected, also, that the room was so little adapted to confine her securely that it could not have been chosen with deliberation. It must have been on a sudden resolution or impulse that he had trapped her there. She decided to wait events for a half an hour longer, and, before this period ended, her patience had its reward.

She heard a light, quick step on the landing. The key turned, and Kingsley came in.

She saw, at the first glance, that it was not the Kingsley who had confronted her with the menace of a pistol muzzle, but he of the earlier day. There was a look in his eyes which was blended of resentment, sulkiness, and shame—possibly of distrust, also. Certainly, she thought, there was an uncomfortable doubt as to how she would receive him.

This was a Kingsley with whom she knew how to deal very easily. Her courage came, and with it, curiously enough, considering the treatment she had experienced, her own resentment died. It was as though they resumed the relations of an earlier hour, and the intervening discord was blotted out.

She attacked at once, and on an unprotected flank, when she said, meeting his uncertain glance with amused and friendly eyes, "I suppose this is to pay me back for keeping you waiting this morning." She imitated his voice and tone as she quoted, "I thought you'd never come." It brought irresistibly to his mind the incidents and hopes of the earlier day. She changed to a form of mockery as she continued, "If there *is* anything left of that $30.00 of food—considering that I helped you to carry it in—"

"You know I don't—" he began miserably, and then changed to a more resolute note. "You can have the lot, if you want. We—I haven't touched it at all. But it's no use going on like that now. I've come to talk straight. Can't you talk real honest for once?"

"Kingsley," she said, "you can't ask that, unless you do it to me. You haven't talked a straight sentence to me since we met—yesterday." (Was it really no longer than that? She was startled by the realization of her own words.)

"Yes, I have," he said, with a genuine indignation. "I've done nothing else. I always talk straight. I don't rag like you. I've asked you to marry me as soon as you like. I can't do more than that, can I? It isn't my fault you're here now."

"No?" she said sceptically. "Perhaps you'll tell me it's mine next?"

"Sure," he replied. "I reckon that's just it. You wouldn't be here now if you'd answered sensibly this morning. And who asked you to stop that sleuth in the lane? If you talk to cops like that, you must expect what you get."

"I've known Inspector Cleveland for about two years, and I always talk to him when we meet, and I expect I always shall."

"Then I guess he told you what's brought him down here?"

It was an awkward question to answer. It might be necessary to choose sides, as she already saw, between the forces of authority, including her brother, and those who were of a lawlessness that she could only guess, but she had not yet done this, and might not be disposed to betray either, even if or when such a decision should have been made.

She avoided a direct reply by repeating her previous condition, which she felt to be of an invincible reasonableness.

"If you mean to hint that I'm not playing square with you, you're dead wrong; but if you think I'm going to tell you anything because I'm locked into rooms, you're even a bit sillier than I thought, and that's saying a lot.

"I've told you that if you want a straight talk you can make a start when you like. And if you want to go on talking up here, you'd better go down first, and bring up that tin of biscuits that's got the paper off on one side. I couldn't say a word more while I'm being starved like this. It's bad for the larynx or the epiglottis or something, or else it's the bronchial tubes."

"That's what I came up to do. I'm real sorry about the food. I was too worried to think about it. But I came to ask you to have a straight talk, and I meant to tell you the lot."

Cora did not answer at once, then she said: "Kingsley, why did you tell me you never carry a gun in this country?"

"Because it's true."

"You know it isn't. What about having one today?"

"I haven't got one. It's at the bottom of my grip at Ellam's, where I've been staying. It's been there ever since the officer put it back."

There was a longer silence from Cora—a silence which did not result from the condition of her bronchial tubes. She was gazing with a singular intentness at a very small cut on his left cheek, such as may be indicted by a safety razor, in a hurried or careless hand.

"*Kingsley*," she said, *"now how many of you are there?"*

He looked startled, but answered readily enough. "I said I'd tell you the lot. There's just George and me. There's no one else in the house."

"I didn't ask how many there are in the house. I asked how many there are of *you*?"

"Well, it's the same answer. There's George and me. We're twins."

"Then it wasn't you that shut me in here?"

"Not on your life. You know whether I'd have done a thing on you like that. How did you spot us apart?"

"Because little cuts on the cheek may heal at midday, but they don't come back in the afternoon."

Mr. Kingsley Starr's hand went up to the side of his face. "You're a sharp one," he said. "It's the first time we've been caught out—when we've been serious." And then he added, "You must have looked close."

Cora made no answer to this. She did not look close. She looked annoyed. Then she looked up with a resumption of her more frequent expression.

"I think you ought to be ashamed of yourself, anyway. A nice mess you'd have got me into, if I'd married you, and then wasn't sure which."

"You could have asked, couldn't you?"

"And how should I have known that you told me the truth, or that it was you at all? There's one thing though—I'm not popular with George. When he pulled his gun on me—that's the right word, isn't it?—there was no real love in his eye. Perhaps it's just as well—"

"I thought you said we'd have a straight talk."

"I said we shouldn't talk at all till I got fed."

"Then come on down now."

"Is George about? Kingsley, I'm not really sure that you hadn't better take to carrying that gun."

"I shouldn't draw it on George, if I did."

"Not even to save the life of your bride-to-be? It's just as well to be warned in time. I suppose a bride more or less doesn't count. Not in Chickadee: 'Give us this day our daily bride.' Isn't that how they all pray in America?"

Cora stopped abruptly. She was a religious-minded young woman, and she was often contritely aware of unintended irreverencies which would articulate themselves too promptly for complete repression. But how *can* you tell how a sentence will end, which may begin with the innocence of a new-born child?

Kingsley, leading the way down the stairs which we have admired already, missed a point that was less personal to himself than he supposed. He was not a student of divorce statistics, and was unaware of the reputation which his country holds in Western Europe.

"I've told you," he replied, with some excusable irritation, "that I've never married anybody. I never wanted to, till I met you."

"Yesterday," Cora finished for him. "Till then you were only kissing the girl that 'doesn't count.' I suppose that's how you describe all the girls that you leave behind. There's one sure thing though. Oh, this is George, is it?"

It was an astonishing likeness, and even though George had changed back into his own upper garments, Cora felt that she would have some difficulty in keeping them clearly separate in her eyes and thoughts. But she noted with interest that that exchange had been made, and readjusted subsequently, so that there had been something more than a casual attempt to introduce George to her in

Kingsley's likeness. Another bone to be picked with him when the occasion offered!

"I suppose we don't need to be introduced, Mr. Starr," she said easily, holding out a friendly hand, which was taken without alacrity "Kingsley tells me that there's $10.00 apiece of potted food, and then we're to have a heart-to-heart talk, and I hope you'll remember that it isn't etiquette in Chickadee to shoot people who don't carry a gun."

But there was no answer from George. She saw that he was not of a mood to respond to banter, and of a hostility which he had no care to conceal. She felt that the atmosphere had changed with his appearance. It was with a rear-guard effort to maintain the conversation on the level at which she felt that she could best control it that she added: "There's one thing, Kingsley—if I should vamp you into the Great Mistake, there won't be any unbrotherly competition to worry you. It won't be a Tragedy of the Jealous Twins."

The remark fell flat. Neither answered at all, but both men looked disconcerted beyond any reason that she could think. Had there been some previous difference between them over such a matter, of which her words brought an awkward memory? She had read that twins are often allied very closely, not only in mutual affection, but in their desires and preferences. It must be tragedy, indeed, when their affections are directed to an object that only one can gain.

For once, not knowing how, or how deeply, she had gone wrong, she had the sense to be silent, and it was not until a somewhat miscellaneous but ample meal had been spread upon the dresser against which they must stand, the window-ledge being too narrow and too dirty to please them, that she ventured to inquire which was the elder, and learnt that it was George who could claim the slender precedence of an eight minutes' seniority.

CHAPTER XXVIII.

CORA had developed a very healthy appetite on her arrival at Cheshurst Hall, which had not been diminished by the period of solitary confinement which followed. She did not allow the meal which was now in sight to be adversely affected either by anxiety as to the outcome of her adventure, or impatience to hear the revelations which were to follow.

Mr. Kingsley Starr's somewhat prodigal purchases had been restricted to such foods as can be confined with more or less permanence either in till or glass. There was bottled beer and milk.

She would have preferred tea to either, but the milk would do. She sampled sardines, lobster, salmon, tongue, with three varieties of biscuits, and advanced confidently to pears and peaches, only calling a reluctant halt when George, who had thawed slightly as a dispenser of hospitality, invited her to a further effort.

"Say, Miss Pratt, is it a can of apricots or the pineapples?"

"Not for me, thanks," she said, and it was evident that it would not be for her hosts, who had concentrated on the bottled beer, and a tin of pressed beef, and finished about ten minutes earlier, although one or the other had been at the window all the time, in apparent contemplation of an ill-paved yard and an opposite wall, the condition of which suggested that the purchaser of the property would soon become familiar with a builder's estimates.

But they had not been studying the wall. They had been discounting the possibility that anyone might enter the yard and approach the window before one of them should have time to withdraw, and so observe the duplication of personality which they were so concerned to hide.

Now Kingsley, who was on guard at the moment when Cora declined further battle with the tinned provisions, said briskly, "Let's go upstairs. We can't talk like this."

"Sure we can't," his brother assented. "If Miss Pratt's quite finished—?"

"I shan't starve before I get home," Cora admitted. "But I'd got some arrears to make up."

"She'll rag me about that till I die," Kingsley said miserably.

"I said till one of us. I didn't say which," she answered. "And if you're going to strangle your innocent victim in the third-best attic, it won't worry you long. I don't care much what happens after that lunch. So come on, and let's hear the tale of crime. I suppose the washing-up waits?"

Kingsley was leading the way upstairs as she spoke, without giving more heed to her chatter than it deserved, but George was at her side, making no answer, but watching her with intent and speculative eyes. She told herself that she wasn't frightened of George, but was not entirely satisfied with her own veracity.

They came to a long attic, with a casement window at one end and another in the sloping roof, from an interior view of which, Cora was informed, Menzies had been defeated by the shortness of the ladder which he had erected.

She saw that it already showed evidence of occupation. There was bedding on the floor in which it was clear that someone had slept, there was a travelling-trunk under the window, and a small looking-glass had been nailed to the wall.

Kingsley took a rug from the bedding and spread it on the floor. "You'll be tired of standing," he said, "and we've not bought the chairs yet."

The queer trio sat down somewhat closely on the floor together, and after a whispered word between the twins, Kingsley opened the conversation.

"See here, Miss Pratt"—Cora noticed, as an evidence of reduced cordiality, that he had ceased the more familiar style of the earlier day—"we want you to understand that we're not crooks, if we do happen to know how Bulfwin got shot. We're going to tell you the whole thing, and you can give us away if you're that sort, which I don't reckon you arc. You can do us in if you want, and you can help us a lot if you're the right sort."

"I shan't give you away," she said readily, "but as to helping, I don't know. I won't promise anything till I've heard it all, and perhaps not then."

"Well, it's our risk. But if you'd known Bulfwin, you'd know that he's no loss. We're not sorry he's dead, and we reckon we're safe enough now, if we lie low; but it's no fun two of us having to be one all the time, and if we hadn't got this place as we did yesterday, it couldn't have gone on much longer. Now we reckon we're sure right, if you'll help us out."

"I suppose," she said, "that that was why I had that interesting proposal this morning? I was to marry one of you, and then swear you were the only husband I'd got. For cool cheek, Mr. Kingsley Starr—"

"You know I didn't—" he began.

"You needn't take any notice of that," his brother interposed. "It was just a silly idea."

The voices of the twins were curiously alike, that of George being even softer than his brother's, and Cora might have thought it to indicate a singularly harmless nature, had not the small round hole of a pistol muzzle been the kind of memory which is not easily forgotten in an afternoon.

"It was that," she said, with a heartiness which George seemed to appreciate more than his brother; "but if you mean that you aren't crooks, and aren't a gang, and have done nothing more or less than shoot Mr. Bulfwin, and never mean to do anything worse, or anything more—well, it's very disappointing to a young thing who hoped to tread the labyrinths of gory crime—"

"I think you'd rag if you knew you'd be dead in an hour," Kingsley interrupted, "but if you can't see that it's no joke for us."

"Don't be silly," George interrupted in turn. "Miss Pratt's going to help us, if you'll only keep quiet."

"I didn't say that," Cora answered. "I only said I wouldn't give you away. I wish you'd tell me more about what really happened."

"So we would," Kingsley answered, "if you'd let anyone speak but yourself."

"Well, go ahead."

"You've heard why Bulfwin came here, and why I followed?"

"Yes, I know all that, only I didn't know that 'I' ought to have been 'we'."

"No more did he. George didn't go to Chickadee. Bulfwin only knew me. We never let out about each other unless we must. If you knew the larks—"

"Go on, Kingsley," George interposed. "You won't finish before it gets dark."

"When I followed him, I didn't use my own name. I didn't want him to hear that I'd come till I'd found out what sort of game he'd been playing. When George followed me—it was he that came on the *Baltic*—he thought it was good enough to use my name. It doesn't matter why now. When I found out Bulfwin's tricks, and he promised to put it all straight, George hadn't come on the scene. It was only that last day, when we found he was double-crossing us all—Trentham, too by selling to Moscow in his own name, that we gave him his last fright, when we walked in on him together. He got so scared that he hadn't the pluck left to lie."

"So you both shot him at the same time?"

"Yes, it was the only way, if we weren't to get it ourselves."

"And that's the straight truth?"

"Yes, and if you can't believe it—"

"I don't say whether I believe it or not. I'm only wondering why you've told me you've never carried a gun in this country."

"Because I haven't. I took his gun off him while George covered him with his."

"Then you took his gun away, and shot him when he'd given it up?"

"We did just that. Look here, Miss Pratt, I wish you weren't so ready to think all the nasty things you can. Suppose we did—he'd got a secret of ours that he could sell for himself, and we couldn't stop him while he was alive, not for another day, nor undo it when it was once done. If we had—"

"I don't think anything justifies a murder like that, and I'm not going to say—"

This time it was George's soft voice that interposed. He had been watching the wrangle with unconcealed satisfaction, but now he said, "Perhaps if you listened better, Miss Pratt, you'd learn more. We didn't know that Bulfwin had two guns. If we hadn't been dead-quick when we did see it we shouldn't be here now."

"Then that's that," said Cora, who had the gift of knowing truth when she heard it. "And I suppose you left separately afterwards, and one of you was seen in the Holborn Empire, and the other coming out of Bodmin House half an hour afterwards?"

"Sure," said Kingsley, "that's so; and the cops didn't know what to believe, and if they don't see us together, they never will."

"And Mr. Trentham wasn't in it at all?"

"No."

"I wish you'd tell me this, if you can. Has Mr. Trentham been straight in his dealings with Bulfwin and you?"

"Yep. He's straight enough, as far as it shows now. It isn't long to judge. Of course, he's keen for himself. The lawyers told me he was just a City crook, and when I'd got Bulfwin roped, I might find I'd only begun; but he's panning out better, as far as we can see. Still, I guess we'll keep our eyes skinned."

"But you're not in with him in anything wrong?"

"No."

"Then that's simpler. Do your lawyers know what really happened?"

"Not from us."

"They know there are two of you?"

"Yes. They've known that all along."

"Wouldn't it be wiser to let them know everything? They might tell you how to get out of England. I can't see that you'll ever be safe here."

"I can't tell them that. Nobody could."

"Why not?"

"Because they won't listen. I've tried twice, and the first time Mr. Morrison rang a bell under the table for someone to interrupt, and the next he couldn't quite catch what I said, and had to go for a train. But he gave us a hint that it would be no use trying to get out of England now; it would be like rabbits bolting into the net. We're glad enough to have got clear to this."

"I suppose it was rather awkward, after you couldn't keep two addresses?"

"It was awkward all the time. We couldn't meet anywhere except in the dark. But since we shot Bulfwin. If you'd stood in a wardrobe for five hours! Now look here, Cora, you're a good sport, and it's up to you. I can't say I've taken this house to live here all alone, and with no servants, and go out one at a time, and no one to take charge. The cops are smelling round it already. You've seen that yourself, and I guess you've been told it too. I've offered you half the cash—it's a fair pile—and you know we get on together better than most. We'd quarrel all the time if you like, and no woman wants anything better than that."

"I think you're too silly for words. Doesn't half the money belong to George? He looks as though you'd have a wife just half a minute after the first time you left us alone, or perhaps less."

It was a fact that George didn't look pleased at the direction which the conversation had taken. He appeared deaf to the advantages of the projected alliance. But it seemed that it wasn't the money which concerned his mind.

"Of course, it's half his," Kingsley answered, "that's why I didn't offer you more."

"Well, I will say you're not mean. But I'm afraid you'll have to think of another plan."

Cora—need it be said?—had a lively mind, and a headline in the evening papers of a future day, THE GIRL WHO MARRIED TWO CROOKS, was very plainly before her. Her brother's association with the C.I.D. had given her some miscellaneous knowledge of criminal law and procedure. Whimsically, she imagined herself in the witness-box. "My lord," the learned counsel was saying, "the

121

witness is the wife of one of the prisoners in the dock, and cannot legally be required to give evidence against him—but nobody's quite sure which it is." Not for Cora. No, thanks.

But, all the same, she was not disposed to desert those who had confided in her, nor was she of a nature to give merely passive support when her sympathies were enlisted.

She saw that if the twins were not involved with Mortimer Trentham in any unlawful enterprise, she could give them her support without disloyalty to her brother. She was under no obligation to Inspector Cleveland, and she had a contempt for the interfering stupidity of the law which is more common among women than men. Bulfwin was dead. He appeared to be a slight loss to the world, and, in any case, he couldn't be brought back to life. To make a fuss about it now was just to give trouble to the living, and to make bad worse.

But she had some respect for the patient obstinacy of Inspector Cleveland, and his presence in the district that afternoon was sufficient indication that he held stubbornly to the trail, even though he might seem to be on a cold scent.

"We're not going to buy any furniture today," she said finally. "George'll have to lump it as best he can. What time is it?"

"It's ten minutes to five."

"Then we've got to start for Orpington at once. We want a good house-decorator."

"I don't see why."

"But I do. How long have I been shut up alone with Mr. Starr in an empty house, with Inspector Cleveland in the back lane, and Menzies looking over the hedge? Three hours, near enough. What do they suppose we've been doing all the time? Menzies can think what he likes, but we're not going to leave Inspector Cleveland guessing. We're going to help him to find out."

"I don't see what you mean," Kingsley persisted. "I want—"

"Well, George does, and there's no more time to waste talking."

"Yes, Miss Pratt's quite right. I shall manage till tomorrow. Only don't let them come without warning me."

"Then you might make it clear to Kingsley (I've never known him as stupid as he's been the last two days!) while I run upstairs for a moment. I think I left my handkerchief in the attic."

The two men stood waiting in the hall for some minutes before she returned.

Then she said, showing the tiny square of lace in her hand, "I couldn't find it at first. It had got mixed up with the quilt when we put it back."

But though it may be a historian's duty to record this mendacity, it is not necessary to share it.

Cora had picked up the handkerchief at once, because she knew where she had dropped it. Her time had been spent in the examination of some articles of clothing which she had reason to think were the property of Mr. George Starr, and which (quite properly) bore his name. She wished to confirm something which she thought she had seen already. She came down in a smiling mood, which she sobered with difficulty as she took the last turn of the stairs.

CHAPTER XXIX.

THE business in Orpington had been concluded, and the car was well on its way back to London when Cora said, "I suppose you really do want to marry me?"

The question roused her companion to an amazed eagerness of protestation, which she checked with the further question: "But you wouldn't tell the truth, even for that?"

"If you'd tell me what you mean—?" he began.

"So I will. I saw George's name when I went upstairs."

Kingsley stared in an evident mystification.

"Well, it's the same as mine. What did you expect?"

"I saw his *full* name."

Kingsley still looked blank, and his lack of comprehension seemed to puzzle her in its turn.

"Perhaps;" she said at last. "it means more to me than it does to you. Anyway, I wish you'd told me at first."

"There's no need to tell you anything," he said, in a tone in which sulkiness and admiration were about equally blended. Even now, he was not quite sure what she meant, though he supposed she must—but he couldn't imagine *how*—

They went on in an unusual silence.

* * * * * * *

It was at this time that Inspector Cleveland was interviewing the assistant manager of Lyons and Hackwell, who carry on a flourishing business as House Painters and Decorators in Orpington High Street.

"Seemed to leave it all to the young lady, did Mr. Starr. A very pleasant young lady, she was, but one as—that knows her own mind, as you might say. There's no doubt" (with a smirk) "who'll be the mistress *there*. Yes, 3:00 P.M. tomorrow, and we're to be there prompt."

Inspector Cleveland was not sufficiently credulous to suppose that Cora thought of marrying the American, he only concluded that she was a better actress than he had realized previously. As to that, all women were. Anyhow, he had found out what they had been doing all afternoon in the empty house. Starr had taken her to look over the place, and to advise on a scheme of decoration. Well, that showed his sense.

The Inspector also saw reason for self-congratulation on a caution which had restrained him from too precipitate action, for he had been half-resolved, as the hours passed, to invade the house to assure himself of her safety. He was fond of Cora, and he did not feel that even her life would be secure should Kingsley suspect the part which he supposed her to be playing as a spy on her brother's behalf.

CHAPTER XXX.

MAJOR CATTELL-PRATT sat gloomily in an empty flat, half an hour after the time at which it was usual to see the evening meal on the table.

Cora—and why on earth wasn't she home now? Cora had been so infernally right about the weather. It *had* cleared, and the sun *had* shone, and the wicket had been—well, what a wicket at Lord's always is on the third day under such circumstances.

Stubbs had had five for forty-eight when he went in, and the captain had said, "Knock him off his length, Major, if you can. It's the only chance."

So he had hit the third ball to leg for six, and the next had come along just the same—or hadn't it?—and he had tried to repeat the stroke.

Major Cattell-Pratt. c. Johnson. b. Stubbs 6 said the score-sheet. Not much to boast of in that.

And now the fire nearly out when he got home, and nothing to eat, and Cora gone off somewhere with a Yankee crook. Well, he could stop that, anyway. What was Cleveland doing that he didn't run the scoundrel in? Everyone knew he'd shot Bulfwin. Probably he'd told Cora all about it. Boasted of it, more likely than not. Women are such fools.

"Oh, Ted, why did you?" said his sister's reproachful voice in the doorway. "Haven't I told you not to try to hit six twice in one over? It always means 'Next man in'."

She had an evening paper in her hand, and was evidently more aware of her brother's delinquencies than of any possible criticism of her own proceedings.

"It's easy to talk when the blunder's made," he answered gloomily. "But you're wrong, all the same. I hit three sixes for the Kensington Casuals off five balls a fortnight ago."

"Yes—club cricket," she said scornfully, "and a shorter boundary, too. You make me tired. But I am sorry, really. It was rotten luck. And I've been having a gorgeous time."

"I suppose that's why I had to come home to a cold flat."

"Ted, don't be a pig. I didn't think you'd be back for half an hour yet. I thought you'd play extra time. You didn't think I'd *expect* that Middlesex couldn't stay in for three hours, did you?"

"I don't see what you mean by staying out till now," he answered, ignoring the ingenious defence which she had offered. "There's nothing gorgeous in being secretary to a couple of crooks, even if they do keep you working till seven."

"A couple—? Oh, I see. You mean Mr. Trentham. I've got to find out about him tomorrow, or Monday. I've been busy with Mr. Starr today."

"What have you found out about him?"

"Only that he's quite straight, and a good sort. I think he'll settle down in England more likely than not. They don't shoot each other up so much here as they do in his parts—look at what happened to that Bulfwin—and he doesn't carry a gun."

"He's got one in his grip."

"Yes. That just shows. Anyway, he's bought a beautiful house, and he's got *perfect* taste in the way he's doing it up."

"How do you know that?"

"Because I've been over there to advise him. He wasn't sure that he knew what would be right in this country."

"And he's going to do it your way?"

"Well, of course. It wouldn't be much good asking me what I thought if he didn't."

"Now see here, Cora, you can give him as much advice as you like. It doesn't cost much, and I expect he needs it, but don't let him start giving things to you, or there'll be trouble. I won't have you getting thick with those crooks, and I'll break their heads if they try it."

There was something in the amusement of Cora's eyes that her brother didn't quite like as he said this.

"He hasn't begun giving you presents already?" he said suspiciously. "You ought to know better than to accept—"

"Oh yes, he has. There's been sardines, and tinned salmon and—oh, I didn't see the potted shrimp till it was too late. But that wasn't my fault. Yes, I took all I could. Ted, if you'd just stop staring like a stage clown, and get up and get the cloth, we might both have something to eat before midnight. I'm just ravenous when I think of those potted shrimps."

CHAPTER XXXI.

"TED," said Cora, as she walked into the dining-room of the flat one evening about three months after her appointment as secretary to Bulfwin's Syndicate, "your little sister's got sacked."

The Major looked up in some surprise. A mutual reticence had developed during recent months, but he had an impression that Cora had gained a secure position at Bodmin House, and though he would have been glad to hear that she had resigned, he was unprepared for the news that Mr. Trentham or his co-director had decided that they could do better without her help.

"Been stealing the stamps?" he inquired, as she appeared to be in no haste to enlighten him further.

"More likely than not. But I haven't been caught yet. They don't check the petty cash as they should. Guess again."

"That Yankee crook hasn't been worrying you to marry him?"

"I've told you before he's not a Yankee, nor a crook. And I don't see why I should get the sack, if he did. It only shows his good taste. You'd see that, if you weren't such a pig. You can have one more guess, and if you don't do better this time I shan't tell you at all."

"Syndicate smashed?"

"Of course not. The safe's cracking its sides. But you're not so far wrong this time. We've sold out all the rights, and we're winding up. Voluntary liquidation's the word, and the original capital to be returned about a million times, more or less. That may be eighteen pence out, but you get the idea. You can't say Mr. Trentham's made a mess of it this time."

"No, but he didn't get any shareholders into this deal. It all goes into his own pocket. He's the Syndicate, isn't he? How does Starr come off? Is he equally pleased?"

"Of course. He's getting his share. Mr. Trentham wouldn't cheat anyone who was inside his own deal. Perhaps that's why he always comes clean, as you say he does."

"You mean he'd cheat anyone who was outside?"

"I didn't say that. I don't say he's the standard pattern. I guess he'd scoop the pool, if he could."

"I wish you wouldn't say 'guess.' It makes me think—"

"Well, that's something."

"—of that wretched Starr."

"He isn't wretched at all. He's in very good spirits. I've promised to go down on Saturday to see how the decorations look, now they're finished. They've been long enough doing them to build a house, and Kingsley says that Inspector Cleveland looks round once a week to see whether he's burying any dead bodies when they put down a gas-pipe or move a drain."

"Cleveland knows what he's about. He's just found out—"

He stopped abruptly. He didn't think Cora would deliberately give him away, but he could not forget her present associations, nor the way in which she came down on any slighting reference to Kingsley Starr.

"Found what?" she said, with a new sharpness in her voice.

"Something I ought not to have mentioned. There may be nothing in it, and it doesn't prove anything if there is."

"If Inspector Cleveland's still trying to make trouble about Bulfwin, I think he might find something better to do."

"I don't agree. We don't want Chicago ways here. A murderer ought to know that he'll always end in the dock."

"Did you say that Inspector Cleveland's coming in tomorrow evening?"

"He half-promised yesterday, if he isn't called away anywhere. He won't tell you anything if he does."

"I'm more likely to tell him."

"I suppose you'll come home again now this Syndicate business is over?"

"I don't know about that. That's what I was trying to tell you, if you'd stop talking a moment."

"You know I—"

"I expect I do. Anyway, the thing's this. Trentham's offered me a new job and a raise to five guineas a week, and I've got to tell him tomorrow if I'll take it on."

"Starr in it?"

"He's got the offer, and he's to find part of the capital, if he does."

"Then you'd better say no. And tell Starr the same, if you want to do him a good turn. He wouldn't offer you such a salary if there weren't something fishy for you to come up against later."

For once his sister was not prepared with an immediate answer. In spite of a conversation which she had had with Mr. Trentham that afternoon, she was inclined to the same opinion, but there were reasons—reasons only partly self-recognized—which made her unwilling to refuse the offer.

The Major had leisure to recall that if Trentham were launching some new financial project, it was a matter into which it was his special duty to make inquiry. If Cora had not accepted the offered position, the most scrupulous honour could not object to disclose the terms in which it had been made, or the information given.

"What is it this time?" he asked. "I suppose it's another finance Company, with a sounding title—and nothing else sound about it."

"No. He says it's quite sound. That was his word. A commercial amalgamation, I think he called it."

"Amalgamation of what?"

The Major was really interested. He didn't expect anything sound, but he gave Trentham credit for understanding the art of window-dressing. He didn't expect him to come out with Amalgamated Dustbins, or Private Airways Limited. All the same, it would be one of those companies that you pass without interest when your eye goes down the list of quotations on the financial page of *The Times*. The sort you wouldn't dream of buying, even if they do flutter upward, and your broker tells you he thinks they're fairly safe to go a few points higher.

Cora went on, "It's to be an amalgamation of all the mill-furnishers in the country."

The Major was not clear as to the nature of the mill-furnishing industry. It sounded wilder than he had expected.

"I thought windmills were a bit out of date."

"It isn't windmills, of course. It's something about belt-fasteners being wanted in a hurry. When machines are at work they wear belts, and the belts sometimes come undone at the wrong time. That's as much as I understood. He was telling Kingsley, while I typed. Kingsley says he didn't understand, and I'm to explain it to him tomorrow."

"It's real business, anyway?"

"He's fixed up purchase agreements with firms all over the country. He's putting up £50,000 himself, and he wants Kingsley to do the same. He says they'll double the money when it floats."

"Has Kingsley got that much?"

"Yes. More. It's my fault. He offers to hand it over to me about twice a week. Oh, by the way, you couldn't have that office the other side of the passage, if you wanted it now. Mr. Trentham's taken it, and two others. Miss Elliot's having that one."

"Who's she?"

"Miss Elliot? She's a typist. She's been helping me for the last month. Wasn't much use at first, but she's come on well."

"I suppose she's the understudy, if you jib?"

"I don't— Oh well, you can't expect them to tell me that, can you? I don't think I shall jib, either. I like the work and I like the pay. I asked Mr. Trentham this afternoon if it were the sort of thing that was meant to end in a smash, and he said it wasn't. At least, he didn't say quite that. He said it was on the square, and I could see for myself, and if there were anything I didn't like, I could throw it up and tell anyone."

"He didn't mind you asking him that?"

"Not a bit. Besides, he's relying upon me to persuade Kingsley to join."

* * * * * * *

It was after a sleepless night's reflection that Major Cattell-Pratt surprised his sister so much that she dropped a piece of buttered toast on the carpet, by saying, "If your crook friends ever get their amalgamated windmills floated, you can put me down for a £1,000, and it's up to you to see that it doesn't get lost in the wash."

Cora retrieved the toast, which had fallen on the unbuttered side, and took a mouthful before she answered: "You wouldn't see that happen again in a hundred years. £1,000. I thought you never risked a four pence. You can't.... Yes, I think I see."

CHAPTER XXXII.

"IT'S a safe rule," Mr. Trentham expounded, "not to have anything to do with manufacturing."

He was entertaining Mr. Kingsley Starr and their secretary to lunch at Gaythornes', and was eloquent upon the advantages of the scheme in which he was seeking to enlist their co-operation.

"If you have manufacturing, you have payday to face once a week, and if it's a big amalgamation, it's a big figure to be found in cash, and you can't put it off, and sooner or later there's a bad time, and you find yourself in the bank-manager's room, and it's 'sign this guarantee,' or 'give us a mortgage on the plant,' or 'what book-debts can you assign?' and before you know what's happened you've still got your liabilities, but your assets belong to the bank. But if you've got a business that buys and sells, but doesn't make, you only owe accounts that you can pay this week or next—more or less, when you like—and they can't get a stranglehold on you quite as easily, or quite in the same way.

"There are other points beside that. There's more profit in just dealing, and you can only manufacture at a certain rate, and if you increase that, it's hard to reduce again. Some people like the Jews and some don't; but everyone agrees they're good business men. Now you'll notice all over the world that it's the same tale. *The Gentile makes, and the Jew deals.*"

Mr. Trentham had not concluded. He only paused because the insistent hovering of the waiter could not be permanently disregarded.

In spite of some tendency to sententiousness of phrase, and an occasional pomposity of manner, he could usually dominate the minds of those to whom he spoke, if he were sufficiently serious in his effort to do so. Even when he presided at the final meeting of a company that he had established with confidence, and that had become a broken derelict in his hands, he would survey the wreckage with such omniscience, would be so lucid in exposition and analysis, that a feeling of vague satisfaction would possess the minds of his hearers, under the influence of an efficiency that gave a vital force even to the process of morbidity in which they were occupied.

But Mr. Starr gave no sign of being impressed by this oratory. It appeared that when he lunched, he did it with an American rapidity. Soup and sole and pheasant had disappeared at a pace that left Cora's healthy appetite in a distant rear. When Mr. Trentham's exposition yielded to the waiter's ubiquity, he only said, "Meaning mill-furnishers don't make?" which was a reasonable, and proved to be a correct deduction.

Mr. Trentham resumed his oration to explain that the mill-furnishing industry must be prepared to supply so many miscellaneous requirements of a modern factory that manufacturing in such variety would be impossible to a single firm. It appeared that there are many hundreds of articles, each in countless grades and patterns and sizes, from pulleys to band-laces, all of which their customers may require with an instant promptitude and many qualities, grades, patterns and sizes. By the amalgamation which he was arranging, he would be able to purchase largely of all these multitudinous articles, most of which could only be bought in small quantities by the single factor, and to distribute from a central stock. He believed it possible, by such an amalgamation, not only to buy better, but to give such superior service as to secure an eventual monopoly of the business. Prices might be cut at first, and then raised when any firms that had refused to join the amalgamation had been frozen out.

Kingsley heard him in silence, and then said laconically, "Sounds good. Where's the ditch?"

"The ditch?" Mr. Trentham was puzzled.

"Yes. I thought your things always cracked up in the end."

Mr. Mortimer Trentham showed no resentment at the suggestion, though he denied it.

"It isn't meant to crack up. There's no reason it shouldn't be as sound a thing as there is on the market."

"And you want me to put up £50,000 before you ask the public to cash in?"

"Not exactly, though you can if you like. If you do, you'll turn it into three times the amount in as many months. There's to be a purchasing and holding Company, that won't really go to the public at all. That's where we'll need the cash. I want you to come in there. We'll clear half a million in six months, if we play the cards well."

"That one not to smash either?"

"We can't talk here. We'd better leave it till tomorrow."

Mr. Trentham turned the conversation to the theatrical programmes of the week.

CHAPTER XXXIII.

ON the following afternoon in the seclusion of their own office, Mr. Trentham explained his plans more fully. It appeared that the soundness of Amalgamated Mill-Furnishers, Ltd., was to be of an enduring character, but its immediate purpose would be to give a similar appearance to the allied company, for which there was to be a different destiny.

He explained his intended financial operations with an admirable lucidity and a disarming candour.

"If we establish sufficient confidence," he concluded, "we might discount half a million."

"And when the last lot of bills falls due, there'll be nothing there?"

"Nothing at all."

"And the banks won't squeal?"

"Not a sound. They daren't. It isn't a game they could afford to advertise."

"Mr. Trentham," Cora interposed, after an unusual silence, "I don't mind Amalgamated Mill-Furnishers, but I wouldn't have anything to do with that, and I don't think Kingsley will either. It isn't an honest thing, put it how you will, and I can't think why, with all the money you've got."

"It isn't a question of honesty," he answered easily; "they'll just write it off their secret reserves, and no one will be a penny the worse for ever afterwards. It just gets back a bit of what they've squeezed out of the community, and puts it into circulation again."

Cora was not sure that she was equal to countering this argument. She manœuvred to a simpler issue when she said: "It isn't a fair thing to do, whatever you say. If it doesn't hurt the banks, it will get the managers into no end of trouble. They might get sacked."

"No, they won't. There'll be too many in the same boat."

"Well, you'll have to sack me, if I'm expected to take that correspondence. And I'm sure Kingsley won't go into it, unless we're sacked."

"That's sure," Kingsley said definitely. Whether he was sure or not of the course he would otherwise have taken, he was quite clear that he would let nothing in the world cause any coolness between Cora and himself at that moment. After three months of incessant verbal sparring, she had consented to come to Cheshurst Hall to approve the decorations which she had instigated, and he had interpreted this, and they both knew that she had allowed him to do so, as a sign of yielding to his matrimonial importunities.

Mr. Trentham had diagnosed the position quite accurately when he had decided that, if he could get Cora's support, there would be little difficulty in securing Kingsley's financial backing. And he would have preferred to have gained his end in that way. But he showed no sign of annoyance. He only said, "We'd better have another talk about this, Kingsley. I might show you reasons to change your mind."

Cora said, "Then I suppose you'll want me to leave on Saturday week?" She felt rather blank at the prospect. It had been a very easy and comfortable position, with a salary that she was very unlikely to get again. Had she been a fool?

"I suppose that's the date." He spoke unemotionally. "I can trust you not to mention the conversation we've had?"

Cora had had no intention of mentioning it, but she was not disposed to conciliation now.

"I don't see why I should promise anything."

"At least, you won't mention it while you're still drawing a salary from us?"

"No, I'll promise that."

Mr. Trentham seemed quite satisfied with this limited assurance.

Cora rose to go. "If you don't want anything else tonight?"

"No. There's nothing else. But I want a few words with you, Kingsley, before you leave."

Kingsley hesitated. He had no intention of being talked over. He wanted to go out with Cora. But he heard Miss Elliot locking up her own room on the other side of the passage. He had his own reasons for avoiding her, so if it weren't for too long....

"Three minutes do?"

"Yes. That ought to be enough."

Cora eased the position, understanding it well enough, and of no mind to go off, and let him be persuaded by Mr. Trentham.

"I'll wait that long," she answered to Kingsley's unspoken question. "I'll wait downstairs."

She waited more than three minutes, more than ten, before he joined her, and she saw at once, by the sullen anger of his eyes, that the interview had not been a pleasant one.

"Come to a tea-shop somewhere," he said. "I want to talk."

"You haven't let him persuade you?" she asked incredulously. "You know it's not an honest scheme, and you've got money enough. It's a silly risk."

"It's got to be done, all the same," he said angrily. And then in a more cheerful tone: "But I expect it'll weigh out well enough. He's too clever to fail. It's a pile for us, if it does."

"Not for us. I won't ever look at you again."

Cora spoke with a decision and an anger that equalled his own, though it was differently directed. She was not merely concerned for the welfare of her country's bankers, though she was genuinely re-pelled by the cool and calculating dishonesty of the scheme which Mr. Trentham had put before them. They had money enough, and in spite of his assurance that the banks would not prosecute, she thought that it was a silly risk to take. Besides, she was angered to find that her influence had been insufficient to turn the scale.

But Kingsley showed no resentment at her attitude.

"I suppose you'd never speak to me again, if I shot the swine ei-ther," he said moodily.

Cora saw that there was something here which required prob-ing.

"I don't see any need to shoot anyone," she said reasonably. "You've come clear out of the Bulfwin deal, and you've got the cash in your own bank. You haven't got to join him again unless you like, and we shall fall out if you do."

"Haven't I? That shows how much you know." He looked round the closely adjacent tables. It was a crowded hour. "We can't talk here," he said. "The street's better than this." He led the way out.

CHAPTER XXXIV.

IF we are to judge by the hour at which Cora reached home that night, the street talk must have been a long one, and, whatever other result it may have had, she made no allusion to her impending departure from Bodmin House.

She was, however, so obviously out of temper during the first half-hour, that Ted, who observed and understood the symptoms, after two sharp rebuffs, had the sense to be silent, and it may have been a relief to both when the bell rang and Inspector Cleveland appeared, with a hope that it wasn't too late for a talk.

"I want," he said, coming straight to the point, "to tell you the progress we've made in regard to the Bulfwin murder."

He observed, as did her brother, the startled look that came into Cora's eyes as he made this remark, which was concealed in a moment, as she said readily, "I should have thought you'd have had the sense to drop that before now. What difference does it make?"

"We don't drop these things, Miss Pratt, till we've got someone in the right place."

"You'll have to drop this," she said resolutely.

"We don't look much like it," he answered, with an equal confidence. "You'll see that, when I tell you just how far we've got."

"I suppose you're sure...," the Major began, and then stopped. His thought was that Cleveland was showing less than his usual discretion in talking with such freedom before his sister, who made little effort to conceal the direction to which her sympathies gravitated. But after all, he must judge that for himself. He couldn't tell him to shut up, for such a reason, in Cora's presence. And, perhaps, if she knew that the murder were about to be brought home to its perpetrators, it might teach her sense, if anything would.

So the Inspector, who knew quite well what he was doing, and would have been pleased to know that all he said would be repeated to Kingsley next morning, went on without further interruption.

"It was that moment's hesitation when he was asked on what ship he came over that put us on the right track, though it didn't seem to lead anywhere at first. We found his name on the register, and we got a description of him from his cabin-steward that seemed to leave us no doubt. But I wouldn't leave it at that, and I found out that if he weren't in London the week before the *Baltic* came into port—and that doesn't seem possible—there was someone here using his name, and someone that Bulfwin met, and recognized as coming from him, if it weren't himself, as it couldn't very well have been.

"But, whoever it was, it's clear that there were two of them, and that explains the two shots; and when you're that far, it's easy to see why he got hold of that empty house. And we've got two witnesses there who tell tales of someone lurking about before he arrived, or after he'd been seen driving away."

Cora appeared to have regained her serenity as this narrative proceeded. "You are clever, Mr. Cleveland," she said sweetly. "I suppose now you've found that out, you'll arrest them both?"

"Yes, Miss Pratt, that's what we shall, the first minute we can lay our hands on the pair. And that won't be long now."

"What are you going to do next?"

"We're going to get a warrant to search that house from top to bottom."

"Well, don't do it before Saturday, because I've promised to go down that afternoon to look at the decorations, and I don't want to find it all messed up. I suppose you'd put it off, if it were a wet day?"

The Inspector looked irritated. She wasn't taking it quite as he had expected. But he answered seriously, "I shouldn't go there again, if I were you. You don't want to get mixed up any more with a thing like this."

He didn't really attach much importance to searching the house, it having been so closely and quietly watched for a month past that he had decided that, whatever might have been the case in earlier weeks, the man he sought was no longer there. Even the quantities of food that were taken when Kingsley was there, as he sometimes would be for a few days, had been watched. More than that, the painters and decorators had had a free run of the house at one period, though their work for the last month had been upon the outbuildings, gates, and fences. No, he did not think anyone was there now. The difficulty was that he could not trace him at all.

Kingsley had been watched, too, by his most capable men. He had gone nowhere, he had spoken to no one, for a month past, without observation. He had received no letter that had not been opened before its delivery; had written none that had not been subjected to a similar scrutiny.

Now the Inspector was making a last throw. If Cora warned him, as he felt sure she would, might he not make some effort to pass the warning on, which would almost surely be observed, and guide him to the capture he sought?

But he had a real regard for Cora, both for herself, and as the sister of his friend. His caution was genuine enough, though he did not expect her to heed it.

If Kingsley's companion were still at Cheshurst Hall, the warning he had given would almost certainly result in an attempt to bolt, which he thought the watch he had set would be equal to thwarting.

He was beating the coverts for a bird that would not rise, but which could be easily seen and shot, if it were once on the wing. Perhaps a little mystery would be best.

He went on, "I don't say he's at the Hall, but if he's not there, I've a good idea where he can be found. I wouldn't mind betting an even fiver that we'll lay them both by the heels before this day week."

"Why don't you make sure of the one while you can?" asked the Major, who regarded his sister's advocacy of the man, of whom he persisted in thinking as the 'Yankee Crook,' with a strong disfavour.

"Because the A.C. wants us to make the case as strong as we can before we move. It's all right to say we feel sure there were two, and here's one in the dock, but it's a very different look if we've got them both to show, and can tell how the one's been hiding away."

He did not give the stronger reason, which was that they were depending upon a free Kingsley to guide them to his companion's hiding-place.

"I don't believe anyone's hiding at all," Cora said boldly. "Kingsley isn't anyway; and he never has. I don't believe that you know that he's got a companion at all. You just make up what you want to believe."

"What on earth you can see in that man...," the Major began.

"Ted," she said, "we'd better understand one another, before you say any more. I'm going to marry *Lytton...Kingsley...Starr*."

The Major leapt to his feet with a most unusual excitement. "That you're not," he said angrily. "I'll be damned if you do. If that murdering crook thinks...."

"He doesn't know yet," she said calmly. She always found her temper under better control when she had made her brother lose his.

"I didn't know it myself till a minute ago. At least," she added more truthfully, "I don't know whether I knew or not. But I know now."

"You can't marry him, if he's going to be hanged for that murder."

"He didn't murder anyone, and he's not going to be hanged at all, and I shall marry him first, if he is," she said defiantly. "I think you men are absolutely horrid, trying to make all the trouble you can. How do you know how Bulfwin got shot, or what need there was for someone to do it, or who he might have killed if they'd let him have time? You sit there plotting to kill men who've never done you any harm just so that you can get your salaries raised, or get thanked by a judge, and you think you're better than Kingsley, who never did such a mean thing in his life." And at the end of this somewhat illogical declamation, Cora burst into tears, to the consternation of her brother, who had never seen her in that condition since he had pulled her hair too vigorously about fifteen years ago.

Inspector Cleveland faded discreetly away.

* * * * * * *

It is a frequent thing for two people to live together joined either by a bond of marriage or blood relationship, or by the mere routines of circumstance, without any accurate understanding of the strength or weakness of the tie that holds them. They are held together as by a slack cord, and so long as nothing occurs to tighten it, they do not know whether it may have the strength of steel or snap like a scorched string at the first test that strains it.

Ted and Cora had lived together in an isolation arising from the fact that they had no near relative. They were undemonstrative by nature. Even to their own minds, their affections were not exposed or tested. Nor was either of a disposition to meet trouble before it forced itself upon them.

When Cora had gone her own way to the engagement at Bodmin House, and had continued an acquaintance which she knew that her brother distrusted, she had drawn the cord taut, but it had felt no serious strain, for he had declined on his side to subject it to any testing pull.

He was vexed and irritated, but he would have said, had he been forced to a definition of his own attitude, that his sister had too much sense to get into the kind of trouble which was now developing.

Even to last night, the idea that she might be drifting into too great an intimacy with Kingsley Starr had little objective reality. He knew that her actions were usually of a different pattern from the random flippancy of her conversation, and it was only those sudden, unexpected tears which warned him that he was encountering one of the basic realities of life, and that he had an urgent problem of his sister's welfare to solve, however emotionally reluctant he might be to face it.

Cora soon dried her eyes when the Inspector had departed. She was inwardly furious at a display of emotion which had come with a suddenness as unexpected to herself as to those to whom she had shown it. She made no effort to resume the conversation.

Her brother, who felt that something ought to be said, but was in more than his usual hesitation as to what it should be, made two or three abortive starts that fell to silence, at the third of which she exclaimed, with some return to her natural manner, "Ted, don't drivel! If you can't stop Inspector Cleveland making more trouble, there isn't anything you can do that's worth doing; and if you go on saying mean things about a man that you've never met" (that was not quite accurate, but never mind), "I shall just walk out of the flat; and if you want me to do that, you'd better start darning your grey socks now, and not leave everything to the end of the week."

"You know I don't want to drive you out of the flat."

"Then you'd better not act as though you did. But I'm not going to talk any more tonight. I should say a lot too much if I did, and you wouldn't say anything worth hearing. I'm going to bed. As to Bulfwin, I wish I'd shot him myself, and I probably should if I'd been there."

CHAPTER XXXV.

THE Major had a bad night, and got up) with the delusion that he had not slept at all, which is usual under such circumstances.

He had, of course, slept for at least nine-tenths of his average period, but he had been sufficiently wakeful to have considered and resolved upon a course of action to meet this provoking emergency.

He was indisposed to take Cora's announcement of her matrimonial intentions very seriously, but he was sufficiently doubtful of his own judgment on this point, and mindful of Cora's threat of leaving the flat, to render him reluctant to reopen the subject to her.

The alternative was to tackle Kingsley Starr, for even a "Yankee Crook" must be capable of realizing the indecency of marrying a respectable girl when under the suspicion of a brutal murder, and liable at any moment to be tried for his life on that issue.

A scruple of how far he might go in a frank talk with the probable murderer, while being on the staff of the C.I.D., was met by an instant resolution to resign his position. A similar doubt of how far he could use the information which Inspector Cleveland had given him was resolved by a decision to see him, and obtain, as far as possible, his permission to do so.

With such plans in his mind, for which he could not expect his sister to thank him, he was little disposed for conversation when they met at the breakfast table, and he found himself encountered with an equal silence.

Immediately after the meal, and half an hour before her usual time of starting for Bodmin House, he announced that he was going out, to which she made no reply, but when she heard him telephone to Scotland Yard to ask that Inspector Cleveland should wait in till he arrived, she said: "Just a moment, Ted, before you go out. I want you to understand that I meant what I said last night—every word. If you can't help, you can just leave it alone."

"Sorry, Cora, I can't do that." He went out as he spoke, having had the last word, probably for the first time in his life.

His first visit was to the Assistant Commissioner, who met his request that he might be allowed to hand in an immediate resignation with a ready equanimity that was less than flattering.

His second was to Inspector Cleveland, who received the news with a less conventional regret, but was equally acquiescent on the actual point of their own interview.

"You say to him just what you like. I don't care if he does know that we're on his pal's tracks, nor that we mean to arrest them both. If he tries to bolt, he'll find himself locked up in something under the half-hour, and if he tries to warn his friend, he'll only put us on the track, which is just the best thing he could do. There's only one thing that I don't want you to mention. You know those fingerprints on the agreement that was in Bulfwin's pocket. Don't let them know we've got that. I don't want any tale they've made up to be squared to fit with those marks being here. It might make all the difference between a walkover and a hard fight at the finish."

"I shan't mention that. I don't see why I should," he promised readily, and went on to Bodmin House, where he proposed to 'have it out' with Kingsley Starr.

He had acted with his natural directness in steering for the only address at which he knew that Kingsley could be found, but he became aware, as he was ascending the familiar lift, while a loquacious Billings recalled the first time that he had accompanied him to those offices, and the sinister discovery that they had shared, that he was extremely likely to encounter Cora, and extremely reluctant to do so.

He did not observe that he was afraid, nor was he conscious of any reason to be ashamed of the course which he was taking, but he said to himself that he hated scenes, and he could not delude himself into the supposition that his sister was likely to receive his interference quietly. He was aware that neither his greater age (which was a fact), nor the wisdom of his proceeding (of which he was equally confident), nor his superior knowledge of life (which it is possible to doubt), nor the dignity of his masculine prerogative, nor his responsibility as the head of the household of the Cattell-Pratts, nor the obvious common sense of the action which he was taking, not all these things, separately or in combination, could alter the fact that Cora had a gift of speech which Nature had denied to him.

He stood in the passage, observing the door which Billings had once opened upon the gory form of the prostrate Bulfwin, and on which a sign writer was now operating to remove the name of the liquidating Syndicate, and he surmised, quite accurately, that his sister was within twelve feet of where he stood, upon its farther side.

Mr. Kingsley Starr—it was less certain—might be there also.

He looked along the left-hand side of the passage, and he observed the door of the room which he had first inspected, which had now been freshly embellished with the name of Amalgamated Mill-Furnishers, Ltd., in evidence of the celerity with which Mr. Trentham was pushing forward his newest enterprise. He had a dim recollection that Cora had said that another than herself—Miss Elkins, wasn't it?—had been placed in control of that wing of the operations. It might be Elkins, or Ellams, but if it had been that, he would probably have thought of embrocation when it was mentioned. Elkins would have to do!

Encouraged by this memory, and congratulating himself upon the astuteness of the flank attack, he advanced confidently to his own destruction.

CHAPTER XXXVI.

MAJOR CATTELL-PRATT'S knock at the office door was answered by a youthful feminine voice, and the sudden cessation of the contending noises of two type-writers. He entered to meet the eyes of two young women who had been engaged in the addressing of envelopes which were destined to distribute the golden opportunity of investing in the business of amalgamated mill-furnishing.

They were of an attractive adolescence, with the slimly developed suppleness which distinguishes the London girl, and which may reasonably be attributed to the incomparable exercise of strap-hanging, in which she is enabled to indulge so freely; but their rouged and lipsticked pertness did not suggest to the Major's cautious mind a discretion which could be relied upon to introduce him to Mr. Starr without his sister's knowledge—certainly not unless he should be explicit in his request, with explanations that might be ill confided.

"Is Miss Elkins in?" he said doubtfully, hoping that neither of the young ladies would acknowledge to a name which he spoke uncertainly.

The nearer answered readily, "If it's Miss Elliot you want to see, sir, she'll be back in a few minutes. Miss Eames is in now."

"I think I'll wait, and see Miss Elliot." (Of course, Elliot was the name!)

"You'd better take the gentleman into the next office, Maudie," the other young lady suggested. "What name shall she give, sir?"

The Major mentioned his name. He was led through a door which had been opened into an adjoining office since he had inspected the premises, to the presence of Miss Eames, a rather plump young woman, who was engaged in typing out a draft of the prospectus of the new company.

He had sat there for about ten minutes, when a door from the passage opened, and Miss Elliot entered the room.

As she came in, Miss Eames rose with alacrity.

"Guess I'll skip now," she said, with more animation than might have been expected from her somewhat ample dimensions, "I've been getting more peckish every minute for the last half-hour. There's a gentleman, Major Catarat, here to see you, Miss Elliot." Saying which, she disappeared into the outer office.

The Major rose to meet a tall, dark girl, who came in with an alert and confident manner, and addressed him in a softly pleasant voice, to ask what she could do for him.

"I wondered whether you could arrange for me to have an interview with Mr. Starr. A private interview."

He thought that the mention of the name made her a shade more distant, as though it were unwelcome, and he had a passing wonder as to what Kingsley Starr might have done to offend this lady, so much more attractive (he thought) than his sister was ever likely to be.

She said only, after a second's pause, "Mr. Starr's office is on the other side of the passage. You should have inquired there."

"It is a private matter on which I wish to see him."

"You will probably find him in, if you inquire now. It is about the time that he goes to lunch."

"I don't want...." How was it to be said? Miss Elliot's manner did not invite confidence, but he had an impulse to trust her.

"I don't think they have you my name quite correctly." He pulled out a card.

She looked at it, carelessly at first, and then with a rising interest.

"You are Miss Pratt's brother?" she asked. And then, "You wish to see him without her knowledge?"

He assented, wondering how she should have guessed it so readily.

There was no reluctance to help him now. "Wait a moment. I will see what I can do."

She went out, and returned saying that Mr. Starr had just gone out to lunch.

"I think I'll wait, if I may," he said stubbornly. He wanted to get this business over, now it was started.

She looked at him speculatively. She was plainly hesitating.

"It's about the time I go out to lunch myself," she said at last. "I can't leave you here alone." (Did she think he would steal the prospectuses?) "Would you care to come out with me? I expect Mr. Starr would be in by the time we should get back."

He was surprised by the invitation, but accepted at once. He would be sure to learn something of interest—possibly of importance. Yet he was puzzled. She did not look the type to make such proposals to any casual acquaintance. Perhaps the fact that he was Cora's brother was considered a sufficient reason. But he felt rather that she had a deliberate motive, and that he must either trust her completely now, or abandon the enterprise.

She paused as they reached the street to say: "I don't know where you'd care to go. Gaythorne's is the best place round here. You won't meet Mr. Starr there, nor your sister. They'll be together, more likely than not, at the place over the road."

He thought once again that there was a trace of bitterness in her tone, as though from a jealousy which was too faint for him to be certain. Perhaps he was to find an unexpected ally, and an easier issue than he had feared. And the girl was lovely! Between her and Cora...What a fool Starr must be! Still, did she know of the suspicion of crime, the shadow of retribution under which he moved? Might he not warn her—and, doing so, perhaps throw Kingsley into his sister's arms?

"Oh yes," he was saying, "just as you think best. Gaythorne's, of course." There was no more conversation till they were seated together, and the meal was ordered.

CHAPTER XXXVII.

MAJOR CATTELL-PRATT, as we may have observed, was not naturally garrulous, and the programme of confiding in Miss Elliot presented difficulties of detail which his first impulse had overlooked.

He had too much consideration for a man in whom his sister was so obviously interested, even though he might dislike him personally, and be engaged upon a mission of separation, to disclose, except to himself, the imminent menace of arrest by which he was threatened, or to discuss a crime of which he believed him guilty; his common sense was amply sufficient to warn him that any criticism of Mr. Starr might be ill received, if his conjecture of jealousy were well founded; he was not prepared to discuss his sister with a lady whom he had only just met, even though he might find her something more than satisfactory as a lunch-companion.

Being so placed, and being destitute of the gift of verbal fluency, it is not surprising that the Major contributed little to the conversation of a somewhat silent meal, though it is difficult to conclude that the time passed slowly, either for Miss Elliot or himself, in view of the surprise with which they finally observed that it was nearly half-past two; on which she remarked that they had better return without loss of time, having already taken about forty minutes beyond the usual extent of her luncheon interval.

Before that time arrived, they had compared their opinions of Mr. Mortimer Trentham, with a caution of words rather than of the ideas which they transmitted, and the Major had confirmed his own judgment, and his sister's verdict upon that gentleman, in several particulars.

He was satisfied that Miss Elliot did not regard him as one who was likely to be guilty of any violent crime, and consequently, that the drowning of his late secretary was most probably the simple accident which it appeared. He learnt also that she regarded the Amalgamated Mill-Furnishers as a sound financial enterprise, very ably handled. And these opinions were of the greater value because he had an impression that she disliked Mortimer Trentham, and had some grievance against him.

Yet she did not say so. She appeared to be a young lady of discreet reticence, which contrasted, to the Major's mind, very favourably with his sister's chatter. She was one, also, who knew her own mind very clearly, and the tone in which she said, "Two checks, please," to the waiter, though it was soft and pleasant, was such that the Major did not venture so much as a verbal protest.

He wondered, as they walked back, how Starr could be such a fool as to prefer his sister in such comparison. Probably when he had had the talk which he contemplated...yet, he was not at all sure that he should be satisfied with that conclusion. Miss Elliot was too good for such a fate. A girl with eyes like that! But it wasn't the eyes alone. Lots of girls, as the Major was vaguely aware, though being one of those men who are shy of any feminine intimacy, have good eyes. It was the whole personality. He had to quicken his normal pace to keep beside her, as she made her way, with a light and buoyant step, through the midday crowd. What could such women see in that Yankee crook, who was almost certain to be hanged in about six weeks?

Well, there was one consolation. If he were hanged, he couldn't marry anybody. Unless Cora were too quick for the police, and got the ceremony in first, as she had threatened to do. Not if he knew it! He had a rather grim expression as the lift hurried him up once more for the expected interview. But, anyway, he wouldn't marry Miss Elliot. The police would be quite in time to prevent *that*. He felt that there are compensations in all things, and it was a resolute but by no means miserable Major who sat in Miss Elliot's room awaiting the appearance of Mr. Starr, whom she had undertaken to fetch from the opposite office, without disclosing his identity to its other occupants.

CHAPTER XXXVIII.

MR. STARR entered the room with his usual briskness, and expressed no surprise at a call for which he may have been prepared by the conversation which had occupied his own luncheon interval, concerning the companion of which Miss Elliot had guessed correctly.

He sat down at her desk, and offered the Major a low upholstered chair beside it, into which he sank with a feeling that he was being placed at some physical disadvantage, which he had no means of resenting.

He felt Mr. Starr's eyes upon him, bright, and wary, and questioning; but that gentleman waited in silence, offering no conversational opening.

It was not the easiest of subjects to introduce, but the Major did not lack courage, however he may have been deficient in conversational adroitness. He came to his point at once, with a direct simplicity.

"My sister mentioned last evening that you had asked her to marry you. It is an impossible thing, for several reasons, and I thought I had better see you at once. The sooner she gets the idea out of her mind the better."

"Reasons?" asked Mr. Starr in curt interrogation. The tone was not hostile. It was simply of a business-like brevity.

"Well, to begin with, there's the Bulfwin murder."

"He won't trouble us. He's dead."

"But the police may."

"Trouble who? See here, Major, you seem to be rather thick with the police. I shouldn't fall off this chair if I heard that you're one of them yourself."

"I resigned this morning, so that I could have this talk with you."

Mr. Starr stared at him in a pause of silence, while he digested this information.

Then he said, "Well, you're straight. I'll say that. You mayn't have my girl's brains, but you're the breed all right. Spit it out, and I'll listen."

It cannot be said that the Major appreciated the wording of this testimonial, but he was too genuinely concerned for the mission on which he had come for it to deflect his mind or ruffle his equanimity. He accepted the invitation, and laid his cards on the table.

"I'm sorry, for your sake, to have to say it, Mr. Starr, but I don't think you quite realize the peril in which you stand. I have learnt a good deal of the police inquiries which have been made, and I have permission to tell you how matters stand; and if you can use the information in any way to your own advantage, you are at liberty to do so. Only, I can't think that you'd ask any girl to marry you while there is the probability that at any moment you may be arrested on a charge of murder."

"Why not?"

The Major, who was not used to doing all the talking after this manner, was momentarily disconcerted by the interruption. It was a question which should not be asked, and which should not need to be answered.

"Of course—" he began. "Surely, anyone would see that. Suppose the verdict—suppose you were to be imprisoned for life—you wouldn't want her to go through life as having married someone who...who might have been hanged?"

The Major had got it out, but he felt resentful at having been obliged to say it. Such things should be understood between gentlemen. But Mr. Starr did not appear to resent the implication. Neither was he impressed by the deduction that seemed so obvious to the Major's mind.

"So you'd call your sister a quitter?"

This puzzled the Major for a moment, and then indignation roused him to an unusual eloquence.

"I wasn't talking about Cora at all. I don't suppose there's a more loyal girl in London, nor a braver, for that matter. You ought to know that, if you know her at all. I expect, if she wanted to marry anyone, she'd do it just the same, if she knew he'd be hanged tomorrow. But that's just why I've come to you, to make sure that you won't let her sacrifice herself in such a way."

"Well, I guess you're right about Cora, we'll shake on that. But see here, Major, the rest's cant.

"As to Bulfwin, I don't mean to get hanged for that dirt, and if the cops could have got it framed on me, they'd have done it before now. If they've passed you any hot air, you can be sure there's some catch, and you can tell them for me that they won't haul much in by that line.

"But as to Cora, I'll say this: if I knew I should be in jail tomorrow for ten years, and she'd promised to marry me—as she did last night—and she wouldn't do it first, you don't think I'd marry her when I came out? She'd be just trash."

"I wasn't talking of what she would be willing to do. Surely, your regard for her own happiness should be sufficient."

"And how'm I to know that she'd be happier, being mean? I don't reckon she's that sort. See here, Major, you're an army man, and you've been through it yourself. I don't reckon you were ten miles from the front. You're the quiet sort that gets through the real work."

The Major looked as uncomfortable as he always did when such allusions were made. He lived in constant dread of being asked to explain the V.C. medal which he kept locked from the sight of his fellows. But he made no answer, and Mr. Starr went on:

"Well, if you'd been kept at the base, and your friends had told you after that they'd pulled the strings that way, because they knew it was best for your own happiness, and that you'd thank them for it after. Well, you know best what you'd have felt. But I'll tell you what I'll do. You can tell me all the police say that they've got fixed up—it's most like that it's more lies than not—and I'll tell Cora the lot, and she'll decide for herself. And I won't say a word, and if she says it's good-bye, she'll be no loss to me. But we both know she won't. So if you want to give her a leg-up, you'd better tell the cops that they can't scare me, and call them off it, if you can. And now, let's have the scare-tale out, and we shall know just where we are."

Whatever Major Cattell-Pratt may have thought of the reception which his first argument had received, he was of too tenacious a temperament to be easily turned from his purpose, as he was too fixed in the traditional ethics of the school from which he came to be easily impressed by the views to which he had listened.

He went on patiently:

"I'm afraid it's something more than a scare-tale, though you can judge better than I, and no one would be more pleased than myself if you could rebut it successfully.

"I'll go further than that. If you could give me an explanation of anything that would tend to remove the present suspicion, I would put it forward in a direction which would be most likely to cause the present inquiries to be called off, and though I cannot say that I should have chosen such a match, I would undertake not to oppose Cora's wishes further, if once this trouble could be removed.

"But the fact is that the only thing which caused the police to delay arresting you at the time was that it seemed certain that the murder was the work of two men, and they had no trace of the second. They felt then that they couldn't make a complete case, and that a jury might hesitate to convict under such circumstances. But they've learnt a good deal since then."

"Yes?"

"They've learnt that there were two of you. They've learnt that one of you as in London a week before the *Baltic* got into port. They've found out a lot about the second man, and they are expecting to arrest him at any moment. You can judge how you stand, and whether you ought to think of marrying under such circumstances."

"That all?"

Mr. Starr stretched his legs, and leaned back in his chair, regarding the Major with an expression of amusement, which that gentleman felt to be singularly irritating. He wished that he were free to mention the fingerprints on which he believed that the police relied to rivet the case that they were preparing, and wondered whether that information would be received with equal bravado. But he remembered his promise. He had, apart from that, an inarticulate feeling that the police had never been really enthusiastic about those marks.

Mr. Starr continued to regard him with an alert thoughtfulness.

"Reckon I could tell a lie, if I tried?" he asked at last.

The Major admitted, with a polite gesture, that most men could.

"Well, I could that, good and plenty. But I'm going to tell you the truth this time, and you can make what you like of it. *The police won't catch anyone, for there's no such man living.*"

"Do you mean that he has died since?"

"I only mean what I say. The cops are just drawing a blank, and the sooner you call them off, the less tired they'll get running round after their own tails. And you can tell them this. It's no use sending any more wires to the Sheriff at Chickadee, nor to the cops back East, where I was raised. They're good friends of mine, and they couldn't say anything to matter, whether or no."

The Major pondered these remarks, but felt that they needed longer reflection than the intervals of conversation allowed. He was sensible that he was making no progress toward the real object of his call. He was already realizing the possibility that he might next be pleading with Inspector Cleveland to drop the investigation, as the only remaining chance of securing his sister's happiness.

He made his last effort in a frontal attack upon this difficult antagonist.

"I think—it is just possible—if you would give me your word of honour—I think that the Inspector who has charge of the case has some confidence in my judgment—if I could give him my own assurance—if you would tell me that you had nothing to do with the murder." Mr. Starr regarded him for some moments in silence.

"Well, I've said you're a straight man. If you think that's a fair question to ask, I'll answer that too, and you can keep what I say to yourself, or use it how you think best."

"It isn't a question I should press," the Major said doubtfully.

"Then it's best left where it is. But I'll tell you this, and you can think it out how you can. I know something of how Bulfwin died, and it wasn't murder at all, and when the police picked him up, he'd got four bullets in his inside, and two of them came out of his own gun."

CHAPTER XXXIX.

THE immediate effect of a conversation such as that to which we have just listened may be very different from that of a few hours later, and this is particularly the case when its influence has been subsequently modified by the impact of another mind.

The Major walked away from Bodmin House in a condition of unexpected uncertainty as to the course of action to which he should be directed by his own codes of propriety or honour, or by consideration of his sister's happiness.

Being in this mood, and remembering that he had promised to call at Billy Trickett's office upon some business concerning the realization of one of his investments, which does not concern us, he decided to put the case to his friend, so far as he felt that he could disclose it, and ask his opinion upon it.

Billy Trickett received him with his usual breezy cordiality. He was a rather thickly built, pink-faced young man with a growing baldness in the centre of his close-cropped straw-coloured hair, and the general aspect of a man who washes himself somewhat more often than is strictly necessary, and avoids any more violent exercise.

The two had known each other from school-days, and when their business was done, the Major told his tale, with some reticence, but with a well-founded confidence in the discretion of his auditor. Billy was no fool, and easily filled in the gaps of the spoken narrative.

It cannot be said that he was an impartial adviser, having had, for the past two years, a fixed though secret purpose of marrying Cora himself, and having been considering the propriety of opening the subject, while in his morning bath only a few hours before; but it would be inaccurate to conclude that his opinion was influenced by this circumstance. By his code, which Mr. Starr would have regarded as singularly contemptible, a man had no right to propose marriage to a girl of his own class (and no sensible man would marry a girl who wasn't) unless he could offer her a secure income, and a suitably furnished home. His own capital had been exhausted in acquiring his present partnership; it was only yesterday, after receiving the results of the last half-year's business from the firm's accountants, that he had felt the time had come when he could honourably disclose his purpose.

"Of course he did it," he said definitely, "and, of course, the 'tecs'll run him in. They don't drop a case like that. You're too sentimental, Ted, as you always were. Of course he did it, I tell you. A man that'd treat a girl like that would shoot his own dad, as soon as look at him. You'd better lock her up somewhere, and leave Cleveland to manage the rest. I shouldn't wonder if he'd run him in for you tonight, if you put the case in the right way. I'll ring him up myself, if you like."

But the Major wasn't sure that he did like. Billy Trickett's pace was rather breathless for him, and as to locking the girl up.... Still, he felt confirmed by that opinion in the resolution with which he had begun the day. The marriage must be prevented at any cost, and it was his duty to do it.

He would go home at once. Cora would be there by now, and he would have it out with her in earnest. He could only pray that there would be no tears.

He would have felt no encouragement had he known that Cora was returning home at that moment as rapidly as the Piccadilly tube could convey her, with an exactly similar resolution. This nonsense, she told herself, had got to stop, and she would have it out with Ted once for all.

There would be no tears for Cora tonight.

CHAPTER XL.

THE evening meal was a silent one.

The Major was occupied in framing and discarding a variety of opening sentences by which he was to strike the right note for a discussion, which he was well aware would not be easily brought to the termination at which he aimed.

Cora, who had no doubt of what she meant to say, nor any lack of confidence in her ability to express herself adequately, was simply waiting till the meal should be cleared away, her brother's pipe satisfactorily stoked up, and the arena quiet and clear for the decisive battle which she had planned on the way home.

When the time came, he was no nearer than ever to a decision as to the way to begin, and it is a tribute to his courage rather than to his intellect that the first words were his.

"Cora, I want to talk to you about that...."

"So do I, Ted, and it'll save a lot of time if you'll listen to me first," in her sweetest voice. "Ted, suppose you wanted to marry somebody."

"But I don't."

"But suppose you did. Suppose you wanted to *very much*. Suppose you wanted to marry Miss Elliot?"

"It's no use supposing."

"Oh, I wouldn't say that. She said she wouldn't ever have guessed that I could have had such a brother. She meant that quite nicely—for you. If someone threw vitriol over me, she wouldn't lose any sleep. I expect she'd marry you by about the middle of next month. Perhaps sooner than that. You know what girls are when they get the chance of someone that's really nice. Well, I do, anyway.

"Suppose you wanted to marry Miss Elliot *very much*. You needn't look so uncomfortable. I expect you will, if you keep on knocking at the wrong door. Suppose you did, and you found that I'd gone out specially to do something nasty to her, so that you never could. I wonder whether you'd come home, and talk as nicely to me as I'm talking to you now."

"It's no good trying to twist things like that, Cora," he answered, with an irritation which was very different from the tone in which he had intended to conduct this conversation. "You know our parents are dead, and I'm responsible for you." (He remembered at least one of the arguments which he had been marshalling and rehearsing for the last three hours.) "If your mother were alive...."

"You'd better not bring mother's name into it," she interrupted quickly. "It's not only that it's a low-down thing to do, but you know quite well that if she were alive she'd be out buying the licence now. If she weren't, it would only be because she didn't really believe that Kingsley'd ever get arrested at all."

This was nonsense, of course. But, like most of Cora's nonsense, it had a sufficient leaven of fact to make it very difficult for the Major to continue to develop the line of attack which he had contemplated.

English character varies. If a wretched convict shall break jail, there will be scores who will beat the hedges with sticks in the hope of capturing him again, though they know nothing of his offence, nor the misery which has impelled his effort for freedom. Yet there are many more who will make the cause of the most brutal murderer their own, will sign impassioned petitions for his reprieve, and will have little pity to spare, even for the victim of his craft or violence, in their sympathy for his own calamity.

Mrs. Cattell-Pratt had belonged emphatically to the latter category.

"Now listen to me, Ted, for about three minutes, and don't interrupt, and after that you can talk all night.

"Kingsley asked me to marry him yesterday. There wasn't anything special in that. He used to do it more days than not, and I got cross if he didn't. But last night I told him I would. I didn't say as soon as he liked, because I knew that wasn't possible in this country. But I said as soon as he could get the ticket of leave, or whatever it is; and that's something under a week, isn't it? I expect you know better than I do. Men take so much more interest in those things. They're not like girls.

"It's no use looking like that. You promised not to interrupt, or you ought to have done when I asked you, anyway, if you didn't. And I'm not going to marry anyone this week, or next. I told Kingsley that today, while you were making love to Miss Elliot on the other side of the road.

"He didn't think I meant it then, but he knows I do now. He came back to me after that pleasant little chat you had with him in Miss Elliot's room, and he asked me whether I was the sort of girl that wouldn't marry him right off because the cops thought that he's settled Bulfwin, and I said, 'Kingsley, how did you guess it all by yourself?' And he said, 'You said it at lunch; but I just thought you were ragging, as you always do.' And I said, 'Well, puma, what do you think now?'—I always call him puma when he looks sulky like that. And he said, 'I don't know what to think, but if you're that kind of skunk.' And I said, 'I shan't marry you, after what Inspector Cleveland said last night, in less than three months from now, not if you sulk till the ninety-first day, if that's what it comes to. Calendar months are beastly things when you want to reckon something up quickly.'"

Cora paused to gaze at vacancy, her lips curving into a smile, as at a recollection which it was pleasant to recall.

"I might have made it lunar," she said. "I was rather an ass not to have thought of that."

"You mean you told him you wouldn't marry him now, because of this trouble with the police? You told him you'd got too much sense, but he wouldn't believe it. Cora, if you'd told me that this morning, you'd have saved me from a bad day."

"It's nice to see you look pleased," Cora answered doubtfully, "but I shouldn't like you to overdo it for me. I suppose you think he said, 'Wretched female, begone!' and so he did, more or less; and, of course, he had to crawl after that. But I'm the goods, if you want to know, and that means a lot in his language. You wait till you see the *Morning Post*, and you'll understand better than you do now."

"Cora," her brother replied, "I never know what you mean when you've talked as long as you have now, but if you'll give me your word that you won't marry him for three months."

"Of course I'm not going to do that, after promising him last night that I'd do it straight off."

"But you've just said that you told him that you won't marry him for three months."

"So I did; I've said both. So I can do which I like."

"Won't you tell me which you do like, then?"

"Yes, if you very much want to know, and if you'll promise to be good ever afterwards, and not talk about Miss Elliot's eyes every evening, till you drive me out of the flat." (Confound the girl! He hadn't mentioned Miss Elliot's eyes. What the devil! The Major was seldom expletive, but we must admit....) "I've been talking sense all day, till I'm quite tired, so I suppose I can do it for a few minutes

more. I told Kingsley the police can't have anything definite to go
on, or they'd have made more trouble before now. We know their
nasty ways. But what we've got to do is just to show them that we're
not afraid of anything, and the more we show them that, the more
timid they'll be.

"All you've got to do is to tell Inspector Cleveland that your
sister's going to marry Kingsley Starr, and what a good thing it is
for her, and if you'd had the good luck to have been born a girl
you'd have done it yourself, and that they're going to live in the
house he bought for her at Little Hempstill, and that she's busy fur-
nishing it now, and that the wedding will take place on December
26th, unless it's a Friday, which I haven't had time to look up. And
you can add, if you like, that you know all about how Bulfwin got
shot up, and no one did it that shouldn't, and it was a good thing too.
And you might say that he can search Cheshurst Hall any day he
likes, if it's fine, and he'll promise not to scratch the paint, and if he
finds the other man that he's so keen on, there or anywhere else, I'll
undertake to marry his uncle, old Briggs, and his children won't get
his money till I'm dead, which won't be just yet."

"Cora, I wish you'd tell me what you see in this man. He isn't
our class, and he doesn't think in our ways, and you can't say he's
much to look at. I don't think he's much more than five feet nothing."

"Of course he is. He's five foot six at the least. You don't think
every man ought to be your length, do you? Besides, he couldn't
help being born a twin."

Cora stopped abruptly, being rightly appalled at the indiscretion
into which she had fallen.

"Born a *what*?"

"Born a twin," she went on boldly, seeing the uselessness and
the danger of attempting evasion now. "But I oughtn't to have mentioned it. He's very sensitive about it, and doesn't like it known.
Most twins are. I mean the one that lives. Most twins die in about a
week. They both die, mostly. If one isn't dead, it means for almost
sure that the other is. You'll find it all in the *Daily Mail Year Book*.
At least, it ought to be there, if it isn't. It will be next year, anyway.
Ted, if we don't understand each other now, we never shall. And if
you won't help me now, after I've put it off for three months and all,
well, I shall just wish you were a dead twin yourself. And if you
ever, *ever* mention what Kingsley is."

She left the sentence unfinished, and went to bed before he had
digested this last piece of information sufficiently to make any reply.

* * * * * * *

He spent about half an hour over the newspaper next morning, while his sister watched him in an impatience which he did not observe. When he it down at last, she asked, with the concentrated exasperation of that half-hour's silence, "Ted, don't you ever read anything interesting?"

Failing to rouse him to more than a formal answer, she took it up herself, turned to the Society news, and returned it to him, with her finger upon a paragraph which roused his attention effectually:

> We are reliably informed that a marriage has been arranged and will take place between Mr. Lytton Kingsley Starr, of Chickadee, Colorado, U.S.A., and Miss Cora Cattell-Pratt, only daughter of the late Major-General C. V. Cattell-Pratt, etc. etc. Mr. Lytton Kingsley Starr will be remembered as the gentleman who has recently realized a romantic fortune in the city, by the sale of a new process for the reduction of platinum ore. Both the young people are deservedly popular in society circles, and the wedding, which we understand will take place at St. Margaret's, Westminster, on December 26th, is likely to be one of the....

The Major read no more. He turned the paper over to see that it was genuine, and not one that had been faked to hoax him.

"Who," he asked, "is responsible for this ghastly nonsense?"

"I don't know why you call it that. It's a bit...picturesque, of course. I suppose those things mostly are. But I thought it was rather sweet of Mr. Atkins."

"Oh, it's he, is it? I see."

The Major had a sudden memory of an occasion when he had been given an orange to keep him quiet, while Cora went to the door.

"Yes, of course, it's Mr. Atkins. I told him I'd send him some more news when I could. But I'm not sure that he'll pay me for that. He seemed to think that it was rather...the other way."

"Yes," said the Major, "I should think he did."

CHAPTER XLI.

"TED, dear," Cora remarked, about six weeks after the conversation already recorded, "I wish you wouldn't keep looking at me like that. I know quite well what you're trying to say, and if you want to know whether I'm surprised, the reply is 'Not in the least.'

"I told George that you'd most likely be blowing in, almost half an hour before you gave her the first call, and I told her then that she'd best get ready to marry you at the same time as I hooked on to Kingsley, and she'd find you weren't half a bad sort, though rather slow, and she'd most likely have to set the pace. She didn't think much of the idea at the time, but she got warmed up a bit more after the first canter. I think she saw it mightn't be as easy as it looked, and liked the idea of pulling it off all the more for that. Most girls do."

"Who's George?"

"George? Why, Bess Elliot, of course. I christened her Bess, because I knew you liked the name. George Elliot's her real one. Had it all her life, and didn't know it was a girl's. Thought she'd been given a boy's name by mistake. Someone got flurried when they saw they were twins, or something of that sort. That was how I found out. Hasn't she told you all this? My, Ted, what a life you'll have."

"Cora, do talk sense for a change. You told me Kingsley was a twin once, and now you say Bess is another. You must have twins on the brain."

"Well, so they are. It takes two to make twins."

"But you don't mean to say.... Cora, I think you'd say anything. It's absurd on the face of it. Twins are almost always alike, and besides...."

"Never mind the besides. That's just it. They are alike. Just. The first time I saw them together, I didn't know them apart. That's why I wouldn't marry Kingsley, till I'd got her into her right clothes. I thought I should be a bigamist in about ten minutes, without knowing which was the sin."

"But it sounds crazy to me." The Major looked at her with a sudden suspicion. "I believe you're just ragging as usual. Why, she's a head taller than he. I always thought...."

Cora saw that her brother was not only bewildered, but seriously troubled, and she altered her tone, to say seriously:

"Ted, I didn't mean to tease. But they really are the same height. You'd see that, if you saw them together, which they don't let you do. It's the difference in the dress. If you knew the time I had for the first month. Of course, I saw the only thing to be done, when I'd spotted the truth. We couldn't have kept George hidden at Cheshurst Hall for ever, even if we hadn't always been afraid of it being searched. Of course, Mr. Cleveland did search it at last, but he was about three weeks too late.

"But we had to keep her there, till I'd got her rigged up with the right clothes—and I having to walk backwards all the while I...."

"Walk backwards? Why?"

"You'll know, if you don't hit it off with her, when you get spliced. I didn't want to get shot in the back. If I'd kissed Kingsley when she was round, I should have got one through the brain. Every time I spoke to him, I expected to get shot in the leg. But she's cooled off a bit since then. I thought she would, if I could get you to call."

"But Bess wouldn't. I don't believe she ever handled a pistol in her life. She isn't that sort."

"Yes, she is; and she did. She shot Bulfwin, anyway, and a good thing too. But, of course, she knows she can't marry you after that."

Cora's voice had a sweet reasonableness as she proceeded. "It isn't that she thinks you'd refuse. It's because she couldn't let you take the risk. You'll remember you explained all that to Kingsley, about as well as anyone could. He said it was just great to hear you, and it made him feel real mean, though he wouldn't let on. You see, she might be arrested any day after the ceremony, and be in jail ever afterwards. And—and suppose she had two or three children after that—or it might be ten or twelve, and they were all born in Pentonville or Dartmoor, or wherever it is. She isn't going to bring the Cattell-Pratts down to that. No decent girl would."

"Cora, if you won't talk sense about this...."

"Ted," she said, sitting up with a sudden straightness, from the hearthrug on which she had been squatting at ease, "it takes two to talk sense, and if you're on, so am I.

"Your little sister's found you a wife, and saved you from being a bigger fool than you know at the time, and if Inspector Cleveland keeps his promise to come in tonight, we ought to finish this mess—except for one thing that I haven't told you yet—before he goes home to bed."

CHAPTER XLII.

IT was two or three hours later that Inspector Cleveland rang the bell, and was disconcerted in mind, though not in countenance, when Cora opened the door, for he was shy of meeting her, since the public announcement of her engagement to a man whom he might find it his duty to arrest at any moment, and she had herself secured his presence that evening by a mendacious telephone conversation, in the course of which she had begged him to take pity on her brother's loneliness, as she would be out until about 2:00 A.M.

"I thought you said you were going to a dance," he remarked, with uncompromising directness, as she stood by, while he hung his coat in the narrow hall.

"I changed my mind. I thought it was too wet."

"Wet? Why, it's a white frost."

"Then I thought it was too much a white frost," she said coolly. "But you needn't mind about me. Ted's waiting to know how you're getting on with the Bulfwin case, and after that we're all going to have a game of bagatelle, if you've been good."

Inspector Cleveland felt a premonition of danger. If he had been got here to be cajoled from the straight path of official rectitude, Cora must learn that she would only waste her time in such efforts.

"I've got my duty to do, Miss Pratt," he answered, in a tone of almost official formality. "There are some subjects that are best left quiet, as between friends."

"Oh, it isn't I, Inspector," she announced, with an unnatural demureness. "It's Ted that wants to talk to you tonight. Men understand these things so much better than girls."

The Inspector only grunted inarticulately in reply. If she thought she could gammon him! They went into the lounge together.

Cora had insisted, with a shrewd effort at self-denial, that Ted should be the one who should put the case to the Inspector, in the form in which they had agreed to present it. She felt that he would take her brother more seriously than herself, and that it was a duel in

166

which the cautious deliberation that Ted certainly possessed to a degree with which she could not compete, was the first quality which the occasion required. And as he had flatly refused to do this unless she would pledge herself to a continued silence, there was a chance that he would, at least, be able to open the matter in his own way.

"Cleveland," he said at last, after they had exhausted the usual domestic inquiries, and the kindred topics which arose naturally when they met, "you know that there's one subject that we can't help having in mind when we get together these days. I didn't like the idea of Cora's marriage at first, but I'm reconciled to that now. I don't suppose there's any development, or I don't think you'd come here and not give me a hint. But I'd like to hear that it's dropped for good and all, and no need to worry about anything that might happen later on."

"I'm sorry," the Inspector answered, "I can't promise you that. We haven't traced the man that we want yet, but we keep on the trail, and we're picking up a hint here, and a fact there; just getting on bit after bit. I'll tell you straight that it's slow, but I think it's sure; and I shouldn't like you, or Miss Cora here, to do anything, and not know how it's most likely to end."

"Yes. I understood that. But I want to ask you a plain question, and you mustn't think that I'm leading up to anything more than I am. I know it's in your hands now, and I know you'll do your duty, and not care for me, or Cora, or anyone else for that matter. But suppose you went into the office tomorrow and said you hadn't enough evidence for an arrest, and you didn't see how you'd ever get any more, would it be transferred into someone else's hands, or would it just drop out of sight?"

The Inspector looked at his friend for some time in silence before he answered.

"It's a queer question to ask, unless you mean to try to talk me over, if you get the answer you want. But it won't be any use if you do. Yes, I'll tell you that. If I turned it in, and made a report that there was nothing more to be done, it's about a hundred to one that it would end it up, unless some fresh information came in from the inquiries already made."

"Then I'll ask you this, and you needn't answer unless you like—you know that for yourself—but I think you told me before that you didn't mean to arrest Kingsley Starr, unless you could get another man that you feel sure was in it with him."

"Yes. I shouldn't say that's far wrong. The Commissioner wants a clear case, especially after this interval. But that's no help to you, because we'll get him right enough."

"Suppose I gave you my word of honour that I know how Bulfwin got killed, and that it wasn't murder at all, and that there wasn't any second man from first to last?"

The Inspector looked puzzled, and there was another interval of silence. Then he answered, "No, I'm sorry, I couldn't take anyone's word for that."

"Suppose it were proven to your own satisfaction that the man you're after *doesn't exist*, and never could be found for that reason—would you throw it up then?"

The Major asked this question with some awkwardness, even some hesitation. It was Cora's idea, not his. He could not avoid a feeling that he was laying an unworthy trap for his friend's unguarded stumbling.

The Inspector saw his hesitation, and mistook its significance. He thought that the Major was aware that he was proposing something, at his sister's instigation, which he knew to be useless, because its conditions were impossible.

He answered the more readily. "*If* you could prove that, which you never could, I wouldn't be likely to go on. No, I don't think I should."

"I'm afraid 'think' is no good to me. I'll tell you this, Cleveland, I've learnt more about this matter than you know yourself—I'm sure of that—and I want to tell you what it is, but there's someone I might put in a worse position than he's in now, if I'm not clear as to the conditions under which this information will be used. If you'll give me your word on that one point, that you won't arrest anyone till you can lay your hands on two men who were concerned or present when Bulfwin got shot, I'll tell you everything that went on in that room, and how he came to his end."

The Inspector pondered again. "No, I can't do that. I suppose the catch is that he's pegged out since. I don't say that won't make it a bit harder for us, but I reckon we should get home all the same."

"It isn't anything like that. Nobody's pegged out in this case that I know of, except Bulfwin. I'll put it this way. You won't arrest anyone, if it can be proved to your own satisfaction that there weren't any two men concerned in Bulfwin's death, or present in his office from first to last on the night he died?"

The Inspector had another interval of silence. He knew quite well that he was making no progress with the case, and it was evident that Ted had some information that might be worth having. But he didn't like the price that he was asked to pay. He felt that there was a catch somewhere, though he couldn't see where it could be, for he was sure that there had been more than one man in it. There were the double shots. Beyond that, there was the evidence he had collected that Kingsley had a companion who had come over in the *Baltic* in his name. Yes, he was sure enough. But what inclined him more than anything else to agree was the thought that if the Major could prove what he said, he was on a false scent, and the sooner he knew it for what it was, and threw up the case, the better it would be. For if that theory failed, he had nothing to go on at all. Besides, there were those mysterious fingerprints on the deed. Useless, if not worse than useless, if they should attempt to set up that the murder had been the work of one man, but helpful, however puzzling, if they could put the two men in the box who must have combined to produce them.

So he said at last: "Yes, I'll promise that. But I don't see how it can do you much good. And I don't promise an inch more. You mustn't blame me, if you wish you'd said nothing afterwards. It's exactly that, and no more."

The Major pencilled the words on the back of an envelope and tossed them over.

"That right?"

"Yes. That's it." The Inspector spoke slowly, pondering the words. He didn't like it. He wouldn't have done it except for a friend he knew. But he was aware of some curiosity for the tale which he was about to hear.

Cora, in her favourite position on the hearthrug, between the two men, looked up at her brother with an approval which she rarely gave him so openly.

"One for you, Ted. He's clicked," she said comfortably.

"I've tried to make it clear, Miss Pratt," he said, with a coldness which he rarely displayed towards a young lady with whom he had been on terms of some intimacy before this unfortunate episode supervened, "I've tried to make it clear that I don't promise an inch more than is written here, and you tell me what you think best at your own risk."

"Oh, that's all right," she answered. "It's a square deal. You never guessed that it took a girl to finish Bulfwin off properly, or that Ted would be kissing her blood-wet hand?"

"You'd better let me...," her brother began.

"We'd better both be quiet, and let it sink in," she interrupted quietly, gazing with mischievous eyes at their bewildered guest.

We have observed already that Inspector Cleveland was no fool. He saw the pit into which it was suggested that he had fallen, and a less reasonable man would have been disposed to kick himself vigorously for his failure to allow for such a possibility. But his mind surveyed the whole of the circumstances and people concerned, all the results of the months of patient investigation which he had directed, and there was no woman in the picture from first to last. He was more than ever disposed to think that he was confronted with some audacious bluff, probably some foolish invention for which Cora was responsible, and into which she had cajoled a reluctant brother.

"I ought to warn you," he said, "that I cannot accept anything without proof."

"You'll have all that; but you'd better have the tale first, and talk afterwards."

The Inspector heard it. As we know it already, we need not listen to Cora's picturesque and sometimes discursive narrative.

"And that's that," she said finally, in a lucid and triumphant summary. "There wasn't any man in it but Kingsley from first to last, and there wasn't any murder at all, and now you know the truth, you can let it lie, and do some real work once again."

"I told you I couldn't accept anything without proof," he said weakly, but he had been too long at his occupation not to recognize the truth when he heard it. Besides, it explained so much.

"You can have that," the Major answered. "There are those fingerprints on the deed."

"Meaning that some of them are Miss Starr's?"

"That's whose it was," Cora interrupted. "And if you want one to compare, you won't need to go far. Ted's just covered with them, about seventeen to the square inch. If you'd seen them last night, in George's office before they left, kissing like two movie stars."

"Cora!" said her outraged brother. "I didn't think you were capable of...."

"Of course I'm not. You know that. You don't suppose anyone needed to *look* to know what you were doing in that room."

Inspector Cleveland interrupted this fraternal skirmish to say: "It seems to me that the most important point you have made is the explanation of how the death occurred. If it could be shown that it was in self-defence."

"Well, what else could it have been?" Cora answered impatiently. "Kingsley hadn't even got his gun on him, and when they told Bulfwin that they'd found out the dirty game he was playing, they just took his away so that there shouldn't be any fireworks that night. That's what Kingsley said. George had got her gun, because she says you shouldn't break a good habit when once it's formed, so she covered him, and Kingsley took a pistol out of his hip-pocket. Being silly, he didn't look to see whether he'd got two. And so they got talking again, and got warmed up all round, and they told him that he'd got to do something that he said that he never would, and suddenly they both saw his hand go to his jacket-pocket, and they saw a shape there that they didn't like, and Kingsley says he had a thought of his friend who'd been shot in the back as he rode out of Chickadee, and George says she only meant to shoot him in the leg, which shows that a girl can be as silly as a man sometimes, though it doesn't come natural in the same way, but her gun always kicks a bit too high, and so he got the bullets where they'd do him most good— and then she wanted to take that deed out of his pocket before they left, and Kingsley said let it stay where it was, or she'd get herself messed up, and they'd better take the guns, so that they could talk to anyone in the right spirit who tried to stop them as they went down the stairs, and they'd better lock up first, and leave properly, and they found the key on the window-ledge, by the bottle of ink, where Bulfwin had laid it down, and then Kingsley said, 'You'd better go first, like we came in, and I'll lock myself in here, where nobody'd come now, and get away later,' and George didn't want to do that, but she saw that it would be safer for both, and so she did, and it was she that went into the Holborn Empire, and Kingsley went off later another way."

Cora stopped from lack of breath, and the Inspector said: "It's a pity, if it were all like that, that they didn't come forward at once, and say that they'd acted in self-defence. It would have been an acquittal most probably, or a short sentence at the worst."

Cora looked at him with an amused derision as she answered: "That's about the silliest thing that's been said in this room tonight. I suppose policemen think that it just comes natural to people to go into docks and places like that to get acquittals or short sentences at the worst, and give the lawyers all the money they've got, and perhaps find that the jury's been a bit dense, and they're to get hanged after all."

"It's every citizen's duty to come forward, Miss Pratt, if he can throw any light on a matter of that kind," the Inspector answered gravely. "You must remember how much trouble would have been saved in the present case, had your friend taken this course instead of denying all knowledge, as Mr. Starr did in his statement to me."

"Trouble to whom?" she answered lightly, being quite unmoved by this argument. "Only to the police, and they needn't do it unless they like. Besides, Mr. Starr wasn't a citizen, nor was his sister, so there wasn't any reason why they should come forward, when it was so much safer to stay behind. For that matter, Bulfwin wasn't either. I don't see what this country had to do with it, unless you say they shouldn't come here messing our office floors, and that wouldn't cost much to put right, even if the linoleum had been a lot nearer than it was."

The Inspector had the sense to discontinue the discussion. "I don't think they'd have found themselves very safe without your help, Miss Pratt," he said mildly. "You'll find it's best to do what the law says, a good deal more often than not. It comes out best in the end."

"How's this coming out, Cleveland?" asked the Major.

"It's a win for you, as far as I can see now; and I wouldn't say but it's the best ending for once, though it isn't often it would work out like that. But there's one or two points you ought to watch, all the same. There's the aliens' registration. I don't suppose Miss Starr's attending to that. If she got caught now, it might lead to inquiries, and you don't know where they might end."

"Cleveland, you're a good sort. I'll see to that. Anything else?"

"Nothing that matters now, but you may just like to know that we've got the hand-marks of both of them on that deed. Kingsley Starr's are quite plain, and, of course, the others must be his sister's, but the way they're superimposed is the most extraordinary—I might almost say the most miraculous—thing I ever saw. It's that as much as anything that's saved Kingsley from arrest earlier. We felt that a good counsel could convince anyone that part of the hand wasn't his, and so the rest couldn't be. In fact, we daren't put him in the dock without being able to show who the rest of the marks did belong to, and so we've been held up from using the best proof that we'd got."

Cora listened to this statement with puzzled eyes. "You say it doesn't matter now," she said at last, "one way or other, but I can't help thinking you've got something wrong. Kingsley never touched the deed at all."

"You're wrong there, Miss Pratt."

"Not after Bulfwin was shot."

"It must have been after that. He touched it with a hand that was smeared with blood."

Cora looked, and felt, both puzzled and annoyed, beyond anything which the point appeared to deserve. Kingsley and George had both given her their accounts of what happened in that room, and they had been so vivid, and so exact in detail, that she felt that she could visualize the scene as clearly as though she had been there, and they had both told her that George had made an attempt to remove the document, and had pushed it back when Kingsley objected. They had even discussed whether George could have left any mark upon it, but had been definite that Kingsley could not have done so, which had been an additional reason for feeling that the police could do nothing while George was disguised successfully by reverting to the dress of her true sex, and had increased their anxiety as to what might follow, should the police discover the relationship.

She felt that, if they had misled her on such a point, they might have failed also to be frank on more essential details. It was a disquieting thought, but she put it from her with a resolute loyalty.

Her brother saw that she was indisposed to accept the Inspector's statement, and saw also the foolishness of such an argument. He said, quite hastily for him, "Anything else, Inspector?"

"If she's still carrying firearms, it ought to stop. She can't do that without a licence here."

"I don't know whether she is now, but...."

"Nonsense, Ted," Cora interposed, "of course you know. Or you ought to be ashamed of yourself, if you don't."

"I haven't thought to ask."

"You don't need to ask. If she's a bit bulgier anywhere than a girl naturally is. I warned her that you'd be a bit slow at the start, but if you don't know *that* yet...."

"Didn't you say something about bagatelle?" asked the Inspector.

The Major got up rather hurriedly to fetch the board.

CHAPTER XLIII.

INSPECTOR CLEVELAND had a bad night. He was man of scrupulous conscience on questions of professional integrity, and though he had felt himself at the time to be making a bargain with the Major by which he was more likely to gain than lose, he was left not only with the feeling that he had been out-witted by a possibility which he ought to have foreseen (which none of us would appreciate), but also with an uneasy doubt as to whether his judgment had not been deflected by a personal friendship, in which case he would have shown himself unfit for the appointment he held.

He admitted to himself, as an abstract proposition, that the dropping of the inquiry would have no particularly evil consequences. He did not think the Starr twins to be of such characters that their continued freedom was a danger to the surrounding community. But that was a consideration which he had trained himself to disregard. No officer of the detective force can arrive at his age and experience without the consciousness that his activities tend rather to increase than diminish the sum of human misery, and that justice itself may be less outraged in many instances by the oversight than by the detection of some lawless act.

They must put such thoughts from their minds by assuring themselves of the value of the deterrent effect of their investigations upon the general body of the community, and with the argument that ultimate responsibilities are in superior hands.

But Inspector Cleveland was clear on one point. Should he fail to discharge the duties of his position in accordance with the requirements of his own code, resignation would be the only honourable course, and whether he had violated that code was a doubt which he could not still.

In this dilemma, he decided to lay the case, as explicitly as he could without violation of the confidence he had received, before Superintendent Withers, in whose discretion and sympathy he had a well-grounded confidence, as well as in the soundness of the advice which would follow.

With this purpose in mind, he made his way to the Superintendent's office, having rehearsed the way in which he would state the case, as we should all be likely to do under such circumstances, and being destined to find that the event would take a different course, which is an equally common experience.

He was fortunate in finding the Superintendent in his room, and that he was ruminating quietly before his own desk, with no appearance of occupation.

"You're just the man," he said, "that I was wanting to see. It's that Bulfwin case. I don't know what progress you've made, but I think I may be able to help you over one of your difficulties.

"When you showed me these," he went on, pulling the set of photographs out of a drawer, "I thought they were the most impossible things I had ever seen. But it just proves what I've observed a dozen times before, that it's what looks like the biggest snag that turns out to hold the real clue."

"You've found out whose prints they are?" The Inspector felt a strange disquietude as he asked this question. Occupied with his own problem of morality, he had assumed, perhaps too easily, and had allowed his friends to do so, that the inquiry would be dropped or continued at his own decision. Now he might have to face probability that his promise had been given in vain. He might even have to walk out of that room with instructions to arrest both Kingsley and his sister, knowing that the duty, should he contrive to avoid it, would pass into less sympathetic hands.

"Not exactly. But I'll tell you one thing to begin with. They're not those of Kingsley Starr."

"Not entirely, you mean? It always seemed to me that that wasn't possible. Though how the others got placed as they did...."

"I mean they're not Kingsley Starr's at all."

"That was what she said."

"She?"

"I didn't mean to say that. But I came to talk to you about this case myself. What I've got to say can wait. But I can't understand how you say that they're not Kingsley's at all. There are two fingers that...."

"Yes, I know. That was the puzzle. It's the solution that it has taken these months to get. I'll tell you I gave some hours of thought to this before I had decided what the solution must be. I was sure then, but that wasn't much use. That wasn't proof. If we'd arrested

Starr on those prints, and put them forward without having the other man in the dock, we should have been laughed out of court."

"The other man?"

The Inspector was not aware that he had put any accent on the last word, but he was answered as though Superintendent Withers had read his thoughts.

"You hadn't thought it was a woman, had you? No. A man is quite clearly indicated."

"I didn't mean to interrupt."

"Well, you know the problems you brought me to solve. Here's a thumb-mark on one side of the top of the deed, and part of the side of a first finger on the other side. They may not have been made by the same hand, though it's about a million to one that they were. The thumb-mark isn't Kingsley's hand. There's no doubt about that. It's about his size, but otherwise it's quite different. The finger-mark isn't very distinct, and it's only the side, and we've only got the front of Kingsley's hand. But it's very like. The lines seem as though they'd join up. The resemblance is puzzling, but it *might* be from a different hand.

"But when we came to the marks that were on the sides of the deed, they didn't seem puzzling, they seemed impossible. There was the thumb-mark on one side, and again it wasn't Starr's. It was the same that we had seen before, as you'd expect it to be. But there were the four fingers on the other side, and three of them were not Starr's, but the first finger was. It was his finger in every line, and you could see clearly where it joined on to the next.

"There it was, and it seemed an utterly impossible thing. It wasn't merely that there should be two men in the whole world who had the first finger alike. That might be possible, or not. There was the fact beyond that that these two men were in the same room, and apparently joining in the same crime.

"'Well,' I said to myself, 'that *did* happen, and it's no use saying it couldn't.' It might occur to anyone to suggest that their fingers were the same because they were men of the same family. But that doesn't help us at all, because there isn't any resemblance between members of a family in that respect. Our records are conclusive on that point.

"'Well,' I said to myself, 'what about twins?' And I couldn't get an answer to that; not at first, because it was something that hadn't been investigated at all.

"I got the hand-prints of four pairs of twins, and there wasn't any more resemblance than if they had been the most absolute strangers. Fortunately, I got one more, and I saw something that gave me hope.

"Since then, in the last three months, we've been on this in earnest. We've collected the fingerprints of several hundred twins, and we've found out something that wasn't suspected even twelve months ago.

"When people speak of twins in a general way, they mean any two children who are produced at the same time by one mother, but, biologically, there is a further distinction. There are what are known as fraternal twins, who often show little more resemblance to one another than is usual among children of the same family; and there are identical twins, who are supposed to originate in the same maternal cell, and who usually resemble each other very closely indeed. Of course, there's nothing new in that. The point's in what follows.

"The result of our investigations is that we find that fraternal twins show few duplications, and very frequently none whatever; but among identical twins it is quite common for any number of fingers to show very close resemblances, even to the point of being absolutely identical in the prints they give.

"You will see that the theory, which I first formed as a mere shot in the dark, is now shown to be little less than a mathematical certainty. The fingerprints on the deed are those of Kingsley Starr's identical twin."

"Yes," Inspector Cleveland answered, "it seems sound enough, but could you tell me why the twin must have been a man?"

"I didn't actually say must," Superintendent Withers answered, with his usual mildness, "but it comes very near to certainty. Identical twins are said to be almost always—I'm not prepared to say that it's less than always—of the same sex. Beyond that, there is the probability I won't use a stronger word—that this was a man's work.

"Now, I'm not going to interfere in this case. I've done no more than give you a pointer, and I'll leave you to carry on. If you find out where Starr was born, I've no doubt you'll be on the track of a very enterprising pair of twins. And if you like to start later than that, you might find it interesting to investigate those two lodgings with this idea in your mind. I won't say but that that evidence, and a few other trifles of the same kind, may have helped a bit in putting me on the right track

"I'm afraid you must get someone else to look for the missing man. I'm resigning today."

"I'm sorry to hear that. You're a man that we can't easily spare. There's been no trouble here at the Yard, has there?"

"No, I've no complaint against anyone, if you mean that. And I don't know that anyone's got one against me. But I came to talk over the Bulfwin case with you, and ask your advice as to what I ought to do, and what you've told me really gives me no choice."

Superintendent Withers pondered this answer for a moment. He was sure that Cleveland wasn't one to resign merely because he'd failed to solve the mystery himself. He wasn't of a touchy or super-sensitive kind. Besides, he had had worse failures in the past, they all had, and taken them philosophically. He had, in fact, so many successes in his record that he could afford to fail without worrying unduly. And, actually, he had not failed in this case. He was known to be carrying on, with the patient persistence which had been re-warded with success on so many previous occasions, and here he was receiving no more than the expert help that he was entitled to expect, and which should enable him to pull it off.

He said, "I don't understand."

"It's not easy to explain now. I came to ask your advice as a friend as to whether I could throw up this case without resigning, after I'd learnt what happened in a way that I can't use, thinking that the truth wouldn't ever have been discovered in other ways, and now...."

"You mean that I'm on the spot?"

"Not altogether."

"But sufficiently to make the end certain? Then why resign? I'll put someone else on it, if it's become awkward for you."

"But I'm not sure that it is."

"Not sure that the end's certain, if you stand aside?" The Super-intendent pondered this, and then said quietly, not as one who in-quires, but as one who recognizes a fact, "You mean it's a woman, and I should be looking for a man."

The Inspector did not deny this. He observed, not very happily, how much more quickly the Superintendent had recognized this pos-sibility than he had been alert enough to do the night before. No, he couldn't defend himself. He said, "I think I must throw up my job. I'm sorry, of course." He thought that he must be free to warn his friends of the new danger that threatened. He added, "I suppose you know that Major Cattell-Pratt's sister is engaged to Kingsley Starr?"

"And you've always been friendly with the Pratts? Well, you ought to be glad for her to be saved from a man like that. Especially if I put someone else to finish it off."

"But I'm not sure that he is."

"You can't make much excuse for a murder like that."

"Suppose it were self-defence?"

The Superintendent pondered this again. He said, "Look here, Cleveland, I'm not going to lose you over this. We've known each other a good while, can't you tell me what the trouble is—*as a friend*?"

"The trouble is that I pledged my word on a condition that I thought absolutely safe, and I got trapped."

"I see. And you're not sure whether you were influenced by friendship or not, and so you've had a bad night? Well, I'll tell you this. I don't intend to let this case drop. If you resign, it goes straight into Hopper's hands, with all the information we have on the file now, and with my own theory of those prints to put him on the right track. But if you tell me anything more, that you learnt in confidence, I shall take it in the same way, and I shan't use it at all. It'll be as safe with me as in your own mind, and I don't think you'll be sorry afterwards."

"You pledge me that as a friend?"

"Yes. We're no worse off than if you keep it in your own mind. And I don't intend to lose you over this. But I can't advise you about something that I don't understand."

"I don't see how it can do any good. It can't alter what I've got to do. But your word's good enough for me, so it can't do any harm either." He thought that, if he could win the Superintendent's sympathies, it might be of some avail in the future, if not now. He told the tale as he had heard it the night before.

The Superintendent listened without interruption, and only said at last, "You believe that's how it was?"

"Yes. I'm sure enough. I'm all the more sure because Miss Pratt told me I was wrong on one point, and I didn't believe her, and now you've shown me that she was right. She stuck out that Kingsley Starr didn't touch the deed, and I said he must, and now you say that he never did."

Superintendent Withers looked down at his blotting-pad in silence for some minutes, fingering an idle pencil. Then he said: "So you're to resign over this, and then I suppose you'll feel free to give the lady the hint, and you'll expect me to start Hopper looking for a man. I don't understand how she comes to be a woman now, but I suppose every rule has its exception, even with identical twins. I suppose you know it won't make any difference? You'll find Hopper will make his catch in the end?"

"I can't help that."

"Well, if that's how it stands," the Superintendent concluded, with even more than his usual mildness, "I can't accept your resignation. If you've done anything wrong, it's a matter for the Disciplinary Board. You can't alter it by resigning afterwards. I'm sending you down to Matlock this afternoon, on this Dalesditch murder. Cleveland, I'm not going to lose one of our best men over this. I'm not such a fool. I've known these little incidents occur once or twice before, and I've noticed they always happen in the winter, when there's a good fire. It's like a dispensation of Providence."

He picked up the photographs as he spoke, and walked over to the grate. He placed them with deliberation in the hottest part of the flames.

"Always a good fire," he ruminated. "It almost makes me a religious man."

CHAPTER XLIV.

IT was at breakfast the same morning that the Major, who had a retentive memory, remarked, at the first opportunity he could secure, toward the end of a meal at which Cora had been more talkative than usual: "You said that there was one thing you hadn't told me... something, I gathered, that we'd still got to deal with before...."

"Before we've mopped up the mess? Yes, that's right. It's the reason why Kingsley went into this last plunge with Mr. Trentham. But that doesn't matter now. It's just a joy."

"Why?"

"Because he didn't want to go in, and I didn't want him to, and he didn't dare to kick, because Mr. Trentham let him know that he'd found out who George really was. He's got 50,000 of Kingsley's cash, and he may make it into three times the amount, or he may lose the lot, but we want to quit, and we can do it now, and I don't mean to have any lunch today till we've had it out with him, and told him to do what he likes, and got enough cheques to rule off the deal."

"It mayn't be as easy as that," the Major said doubtfully. "You can't always get money back in a few hours, even when it's invested in a safe way. Not in large amounts like that. Do you know how it's been spent?"

"It hasn't been spent at all. It's just lying in different banks, here and there. Oh, we'll get it back all right. You'll see."

"I daresay you will, if that's so, but I can't see now it was to make such a profit, if it's not being used at all."

"Oh, it's being used right enough, and a lot more of Mr. Trentham's in the same way. He only wanted it to be in different banks, and be moved round. That was what it was for."

The Major felt that there was something rather unusual in that method of producing fortune, though his laboriously gathered financial knowledge suggested several more or less legitimate explanations, which he thought his sister might be less able to follow.

"I daresay," he remarked, "it's to cover margins. It may be all right, if so. Mr. Trentham knows how to come in when it rains. But I can't see him handing it all back in a couple of hours."

"Oh, he'll do that. It isn't to cover margins it's being used. It's to get the banks to discount due bills."

The Major pondered this singular method of wooing fortune.

"I don't quite see....," he began doubtfully.

"Well, I do. That's because Mr. Trentham explained it all to Kingsley and me, and when he's explained anything one can't help understanding. He told us there's going to be a most awful row in the end, but the banks won't dare to squeal—not out loud, that is—because they won't want everyone to get to know how it's done."

The Major did not seek to penetrate further into the mystery of Mr. Trentham's financial methods. He remembered that he had resigned some weeks ago.

He only said: "Well, I warned you not to go to Bodmin House, all along. You'd better tell Kingsley to get out what he can, but to cut loose at any price, even if he has to let some of it go."

"Oh, I shan't let him do that. You'd better come along, and see how it pans out. And we'll have George along too. She might come in handy with that gun."

In some bewilderment as to how far his sister was serious, which was not an infrequent condition of his mind, the Major came.

CHAPTER XLV.

MR. TRENTHAM received them with his usual benignant and slightly pompous courtesy.

"I don't quite understand," he remarked genially, when Cora introduced her brother, and Kingsley, and Miss Starr (as we must now call her for the brief interval before she will pass into the Major's possession), into the room which we first observed as the scene of Mr. Bulfwin's abrupt decease, with the obvious information that they would like to see him together. "I don't quite understand whether this is a business interview—I remember that the Major has got a few shares in Amalgamated Mill-Furnishers, but I see they're at thirty-six this morning, so I don't suppose there's any complaint about *them*—or whether it's to give me an opportunity of congratulating you all upon pairing off so successfully. But, anyway, I've got half an hour to spare, and I expect that will be all we shall need."

"It's a business interview, right enough," Kingsley answered, "though I won't say that we mightn't have managed it by ourselves, as I'm the one that's got the cash to draw. The fact is," he said, coming to the point with his usual celerity, "I want to cash out. I don't mind the Mill-Furnishing shares for a time. I know there's an open market for them, and I can sell when I choose; but I want the 50,000, and to drop clean out of that deal."

Mr. Trentham showed no sign of resentment, or of surprise. Nor did he suggest that any inconsequences might follow this precipitate retreat. He had, among other Napoleonic qualities, the gift of estimating the probabilities of a strategic position without the crudity of explanation.

He stroked his chin as he answered slowly: "You put up 50,000, and I put up sixty-two. There's no one else in—at this end. We've spent about seven thousand in expenses up to the end of last month. How much do you ask for me to buy you out?"

"I don't want any profit," Kingsley answered. "I want my fifty."

"Do you call that a fair thing to ask, Major Cattell-Pratt?" Mr. Trentham asked, with formality.

The Major was not quick to reply. He was not quite sure that it was. Rather than haggle, he would have knocked off a few thousand as Kingsley's share of those mysterious expenses, and been content to come out clean with the rest, but Cora took up the reply.

"I don't think Kingsley ought to pay any expenses. He didn't really want to go in at all."

"There's a good deal in that," Mr. Trentham admitted readily. "You've always got a clear head, Miss Pratt. I don't think Mr. Starr need worry much about the money, if he's got you."

He gave Cora his friendliest smile. She knew that she could have been not merely one of the Brighton weekenders, but the first Mrs. Mortimer Trentham, had she wished. It was something that she did not mention, either to her brother or Kingsley, for reasons which she would have found difficult to explain, even to herself, but she was very unlikely to grow tired in any effort to do so.

"But still," he went on, "it's a large sum to find at short notice. How much will you take, Mr. Kingsley, to part friends, and how soon must it be?"

"He wants £50,000," Cora interposed quickly, lest there should be some concession if she were silent. "He wants it now."

"We won't haggle," Mr. Trentham answered generously. He made some calculations on a sheet of paper before him. He consulted a diary containing cabalistic figures, the key to which he carried in his own mind. He wrote out three cheques.

He sat silent for a moment, and then drew up a form of receipt.

He passed it to the Major for his approval. "I suppose you're the financial adviser to this group?"

The Major passed the receipt on to Mr. Starr. It seemed simple and clear.

"I suppose there's no doubt of the cheques?" he said bluntly, before he signed.

Mr. Trentham smiled slightly. He handed Cora the cheques. "You might verify the balances, Miss Pratt, from your own books."

Mr. Starr was ready to sign, but he needed a stamp. Mr. Trentham could oblige him. He accepted two pence with gravity.

Were the ladies wishing to leave today? It would be awkward, but he did not wish anyone to stay to their own inconvenience. With the great events so near. He could only thank them for all they had done. He shook hands all round, and they walked out.

It had not been quite what they expected. They had the feeling of a class that has been dismissed from an ill-said lesson, only exempt from punishment through the teacher's kindness.

"I shouldn't lose any time in getting those cheques cleared," said the Major.

"There's no worry about that," Cora answered confidently. "You don't know Mr. Trentham yet. I'm not sure that any of us does."

That gentleman still sat in his office. He had drawn a small ledger from a locked drawer, and was neatly cancelling his partnership account with Mr. Kingsley Starr. The truth was that the money had served its purpose. He would willingly have given Kingsley an extra ten thousand to get him out, had it been necessary to do so. He considered that it could scarcely have happened better. He looked to clear a tenth of a million, and Kingsley would have had a third. With the risk of something worse than a row? Yes, but his risk was the same, whether Kingsley were in it with him or not. And the money had served its use.

He would have wished, in any case, to draw out some of these fast-accumulating balances. It was convenient in every way to pay Kingsley out at this stage. He supposed, correctly enough, that they had found some way of squaring the police, and that Kingsley resented the gentle pressure which had been put upon him to come in. That had been a regrettable necessity. His money had been essential at the start. Not that he would have given them away, under any circumstances. But it had done no harm for them to have been afraid lest he might. It was a nuisance about Cora Pratt. Brains and looks, and a good nerve. Not an easy combination to find...and the time coming when she might have been of some real use.

He rang for one of the assistant typists, and commenced to deal with the morning letters.

Three weeks later, the report of an inspector of more than average intelligence was causing the first stir of uneasiness in the office of the general manager of one of the leading banks. But the Great Trentham Coup, as it came to be called in the inner circles of London banking, is another story. It must wait its time.

Bank directors might study collated lists of floating acceptances and depleted balances, with worried brows: they might dictate letters to provincial managers which would be productive of sleepless vigils for those to whom they wrote. But Cora cared for none of these things.

She sat on the hearthrug, comfortably oblivious of the December sleet that was beating against the outside of the curtained windows.

"I don't think we'll give up this flat, Ted, if you don't mind. We'll keep it for both of us to use when we come up to town."

The Major said nothing to that. He might do so when he had spent a careful hour in calculating the expense involved, or he might have too much sense to waste his mental energy on that which would be decided by higher powers.

Cora gazed thoughtfully into the fire. Her mind was on a coat of soft-coloured green nappa, trimmed with Chinese Leopard-Cat fur, at which she had been looking that afternoon. Would it suit her better than the squirrel coat that Kingsley had got for her on approval yesterday, and that must be sent back tomorrow, if she did not keep it? It was a momentous question, and she could always think best if she were talking about something else, so that she would be secure against any serious interruption.

What she said was, "So you didn't get George that gun licence after all?"

"Cleveland didn't think, under all the circumstances, that it might be quite wise."

"Yes, I've heard all that. I'm going to write him an anonymous letter to tell him where to look, and make her wear it where he can't help seeing the bulge. I think, in the language of my chosen spouse, I'd better put Mr. Atkins wise. He ought to pay well for that. 'Scene at St. Margaret's this morning. Bride arrested by the best man'. That ought to make a rattling good photo; and 'The Major Bailing the Bride' ought to be good for half a page of the *Daily Camera*. I expect you'll have to pay a lot. It'll be rather fun to see now you'll shell out to make sure that she isn't locked up for the night. She's just the one to pull a gun on you if you don't look any too willing. You'd better practise before a glass. What's the biggest penalty for an alien carrying firearms? But she wouldn't be an alien then. You ought to make something of that. What's the penalty for an ex-alien, who hadn't been an alien for the last hour, having carried firearms when she once was? With all the time you had in the force, you ought to be able to answer a little question like that."

"I do wish," said the exasperated Major, "that you wouldn't rag all the time."

ABOUT THE AUTHOR

SYDNEY FOWLER WRIGHT (1874-1965) penned over seventy volumes of science fiction, fantasy, classic mysteries, historical novels, poetry, and non-fiction, many of them being published by the Borgo Press Imprint of Wildside Press.